Giving Thanks

Thanksgiving Stories that touch
your heart and feed your soul.

On Newsstands Now:

TRUE STORY
and
TRUE CONFESSIONS
Magazines

True Story and *True Confessions* are the world's largest and best-selling women's romance magazines. They offer true-to-life stories to which women can relate.

Since 1919, the iconic *True Story* has been an extraordinary publication. The magazine gets its inspiration from the hearts and minds of women, and touches on those things in life that a woman holds close to her heart, like love, loss, family and friendship.

True Confessions, a cherished classic first published in 1922, looks into women's souls and reveals their deepest secrets.

To subscribe, please visit our website:
www.TrueRenditionsLLC.com or call **(212) 922-9244**

To find the TRUES at your local store, please visit:
www.WheresMyMagazine.com

Giving
Thanks

Thanksgiving Stories that touch
your heart and feed your soul.

From the Editors
Of *True Story* And
True Confessions

Published by True Renditions, LLC

True Renditions, LLC
105 E. 34th Street, Suite 141
New York, NY 10016

Copyright @ 2013 by True Renditions, LLC

ISBN: 978-1-938877-86-5

Visit us on the web at www.truerenditionsllc.com.

Contents

STRANGERS SAVED OUR THANKSGIVING
How their gift helped my family

There won't be a whole lot to be thankful for on this holiday, I thought as I watched my house and everything I owned go up in flames. It was two weeks from Thanksgiving.

"What rotten timing," I muttered to myself, as if there's ever a good time for a fire.

"What did you say, Mommy?" Joy, my five year old, looked up at me, and I hugged her close.

Her little cheeks were darkened with smoke, but the EMTs had checked her out and told me she was fine. My son, Sam, had been treated for smoke inhalation, too, but he'd be fine as well. As soon as I could, I'd go the hospital to be with him. But as the roof caved in on my garage, I realized I didn't even have a car anymore. I'd have to walk to the hospital. My raggedy nightgown, the one I wore because it was warm and comfortable and no one would see it anyway, didn't have any pockets to hold money. That was all up in flames, too. I couldn't even catch a bus.

A police officer walked over to me. Touching his cap lightly, he asked if I needed a ride somewhere.

"The hospital, I guess. We don't have anywhere else to go."

I suppose my sadness showed, because he put a hand on my shoulder in comfort. That small gesture from a total stranger nearly reduced me to tears, but somehow, I kept my sorrow inside. I think the fact I was still in shock helped.

"Fluffles!" Joy's cry of delight cut through the fog that had taken over my brain as my daughter tried to catch a streak of light that whizzed by her bare legs. My first thought was how badly my child needed a new, longer nightgown, my second, that our cat had somehow survived the fire. She ran under a nearby police car. Joy broke from my grasp and ran after the terrified cat. Putting her face to the asphalt, she soon coaxed her pet out and cradled her in her arms. The officer observing the scene quickly shut both cat and child in the backseat of his squad car in an effort to keep them both safe.

Wearily, I wondered where our dog was. The flames roared through our house, fire hoses pouring water onto every square inch and seeming to have no effect. I shuddered, thinking of our beloved mutt in that conflagration. The thought sickened me. The children

1

would be devastated to lose Moonie. So would I.

Overwhelmed, I felt my legs give out and I abruptly sat down on the pavement. The officer who had helped Joy retrieve the cat hurried over, concern etched on his kind face. "Are you okay, ma'am?" I saw him glance up, then motion for the EMT still there with the second ambulance standing by. She hurried over and began taking my pulse, listening to my heart. I knew I wasn't going to die. I just had suddenly been overtaken by the sheer enormity of our losses that night. I could see there would be nothing left to salvage. The house was going to burn to the ground. Everything in it would be lost as well.

We'd barely moved into the place. Our lives hadn't been easy. We'd spent more than our share of time in homeless shelters, bouncing from place to place as I'd tried to get my feet under me and provide for my children. Their father had died young, the victim of a drunk driver six months before Sam's birth. We had both worked hard to provide for our family, but I'd had Joy young and had never even completed high school.

With no extended family on either side, after Carl's death, I'd found myself completely alone in the world with two small children, no job, no education, and no possibilities on the horizon. We'd bounced from place to place, staying with one friend or another after being evicted from our apartment. I was so young that I hadn't been able to handle what little money I did get, and the expenses for the children seemed to eat up everything no matter how hard I tried to hang onto it.

The first time we ended up in a shelter, I begged for help. The people were nice, but they couldn't do much for us besides provide temporary shelter. They did help me get my GED though, and they steered me toward a tech school where I could earn a degree in computer graphics and web design. I'd managed to keep up my car payments, and we lived out of the car from time to time, but of course that was an impossible situation, even when I used some of our meager resources to buy us a tent so we could at least have some kind of home. That tent, humble though it was, got us through the worst of things. We lived in it for several months. The park ranger wasn't supposed to let us stay more than a few days, but she turned a blind eye after seeing we kept our space spotless, and that I watched my children and took good care of them. I think she figured out fairly fast what desperate straits we were in, and eventually, she even stopped accepting money for the campsite rental.

Looking back, our time in the tent wasn't so bad. We had a place to shower and go to the bathroom using the park's facilities. It was a beautiful wilderness setting to live in, all within a few miles of the small town we'd ended up in. I tried to present it as an adventure to

2

the kids, and they'd accepted it as such. They'd been so little then, and they had all the important things in life: a mom who loved them, enough to eat, and a warm, dry place to sleep. I was doing the best I could, and I knew our situation would only be temporary.

After I graduated from the tech school, I'd found a job not far from the park where we'd stayed all those months. One of those new dot-coms had started up and needed a lot of technical staff fast. I got in on the ground floor and started making real money. My first check enabled us to pack up the tent and move into a nice apartment. Luckily, I hadn't spent too much on furniture for it, trying to be cautious with our money. The company folded after only a few months in business. I was out of work then, and my meager savings rapidly dwindled to nothing.

Jobs were hard to come by in our area, even with my new education. Most places wanted college graduates or at least people with more experience than I had. Soon we found ourselves on the streets again.

I hated it in shelters. We were better off in our tent. But winter had set in, and there was no way to live in a tent with two small children. Eventually, I found a job and went back to work. It didn't pay much, but it helped us get into an apartment again. It was cramped and not too nice, but we made it our home. I knew things would get better. I never gave up looking for a computer job, but our area had a very stable workforce. Once people got into a job, they tended not to leave it, so things didn't open up as often as they might in other places.

I heard about a program that helped provide housing to people like me, people willing to work hard. I could get a no-interest loan, they told me, with low monthly payments. I'd have to work for hours on the place, but others would volunteer to help me. It all seemed like a dream, but before we knew it, we were moving into our very own house. At last, the kids had bedrooms! We could breathe again. I knew we could make it, and I felt blessed for having been given the opportunity.

And now, I watched all I'd worked for going up in smoke. The tears came, but I stifled my sobs as the paramedic murmured soothing words. The officer, his hand on my shoulder again, asked me if he could give me a ride to the hospital to be with Sam. I nodded, completely numb. It would all sink in later, I felt sure, and then the pain of loss would really begin.

The kindness of people touched me. First the police and paramedics, and then the hospital staff. After checking on Sam and finding him asleep, I sank wearily into the chair by his bed, Joy on my lap. I'd just decided to adopt an attitude of thinking about everything tomorrow when a nurse padded silently into the room. Laying a stack of clothing on the wheeled table against the wall, she whispered, "There's a shower down the hall you and your little girl can use. Here are some clean clothes. You'd probably feel better once you're cleaned up."

Truer words were never spoken, and I accepted her offer eagerly. Once Joy and I were cleaned and dressed, we did feel better. We returned to Sam's room to find two cots made up for us. Gratefully, I tucked my daughter into one of them and myself into the other. I allowed no thoughts of my losses that night, dropping instead into instant, merciful sleep.

The next day was filled with forms, most of the insurance variety. The good news about my house insurance was it would give me the full market value of the house, which was more than I'd paid for it. The bad news was there wouldn't be enough money to rebuild the house as it had been after I paid off the mortgage.

A call came from a local veterinarian's office. Moonie had been found! He was hospitalized at the vet's with a burn on his shoulder, but he was expected to make a full recovery. We all smiled when we heard that news. All of our family had survived the fire.

Social services came and told us they had found a shelter where we could stay till we decided what to do.

The car insurance rep came and cut me a check for my ruined car.

By noon, I was mentally exhausted. It was impossible to believe that twenty-four hours before, we'd been sitting down to lunch in our cheerful little house. Now, it was all gone.

Suddenly, I couldn't talk to anyone about the fire. I just had to get out of there. Taking Joy, we walked the six blocks to our house. Nothing was left but a pile of ash and charred lumber. Any hope I'd been harboring that we'd be able to salvage something died.

Our walk back to the hospital was not a happy one.

A week went by and depression set in. My usual enthusiasm for Thanksgiving and the holiday season had completely disappeared. We stayed at the shelter because it almost felt like home, something familiar, but I still hated it. It was all I could do to drag myself out of bed every morning, drop the kids off at day-care, and go to my job. I functioned on autopilot. My brain simply shut down.

"Darcy, let's have lunch." My friend, Melissa, had been a rock through this ordeal, never wavering in her support, providing me with a cheerful face when I needed it, and listening somberly to my problems when I needed that.

"Sure," I said woodenly. Nothing interested me less than food, but what the heck.

I should've seen the ambush coming, would have if I hadn't withdrawn so far inside myself.

"Darcy, how long is this going to go on?"

"What?" I asked warily.

"This moping."

"Moping! How would you feel if you lost everything?" My voice rose in the crowded restaurant and people turned our way.

"I understand, but you have two kids. You have to come up with some sort of plan to get out of the shelter and back into a real home."

"I will, as soon as the insurance money comes in. And that won't happen till the fire marshal finishes the investigation."

"Have you talked to either the insurance people or the fire marshal?"

"No. They'll call me."

Melissa just cocked an eyebrow.

"Well, they will!" I argued.

She crossed her arms on her chest. She and I both knew this mess was never going to solve itself. I dreaded the thought of confronting people, but I knew I had to if I ever wanted any action.

I gave in. "I'll call the fire marshal today." I sipped my cola, but Melissa didn't uncross her arms. "What now?"

"You're living in a shelter, Darcy. What's wrong with that picture?"

"I can't do anything about that now."

"Have you talked to anyone about replacing your home?"

"I can't. There won't be enough money to rebuild."

I didn't think it was possible for Melissa's eyebrow to arch any higher, but it seemed about to disappear into her hairline. Over the noise of the restaurant conversation, I could just barely hear her whisper, "Chicken!" I knew she wasn't talking about the food.

"You really tick me off, Melissa. I just lost my house a week ago. What do you expect of me?"

"I expect you to get off your whiny butt and fix things."

Only Melissa could talk to me that way, but even she had pushed too far. Miffed, I stormed out of the restaurant. I didn't talk to her the rest of the day, not even when she arrived back at work with a small bouquet of flowers as an apology.

But that night after work, I mulled over the conversation. Melissa had delivered her opinion in her usual blunt manner, but she made a lot of sense. Here I was, a single parent with two little people depending on me and no one to help me. So far, I'd drifted through life hoping things would improve for me. In some ways they had, but only because other people had directed me, not because I'd ever taken the bull by the horns and forced action. Before I went to sleep, I decided to take the next day off and see what I could get accomplished.

I called the fire marshal and explained our situation. Our insurance wouldn't pay for temporary housing. The shelter wouldn't allow us to stay there much longer. Our pets, whom we all missed, were being boarded at a kennel where my children, who had already lost everything, could rarely see them. He promised to expedite our investigation. The preliminary reports looked like it was a case of faulty wiring, he said. The final report should be at the insurance office by the end of the week.

As I hung up the phone, I wondered how long that paperwork would've sat on his desk if not for my prodding.

It was harder to get anything out of the insurance rep, but at least I did get some hard figures instead of vague numbers, and then I knew what I had to work with. I called the bank and made an appointment with a loan officer, feeling a bit queasy sailing through all these uncharted waters. But my children were counting on me, and I was counting on me, too. "A house by Thanksgiving," became my mantra that day. I knew it would take a miracle to pull that off.

The banker wasn't too encouraging, though he was kind. He'd worked in the mortgage department a long time. He went over my mortgage account, showed me in detail how much of the insurance money would have to go to pay off the existing mortgage on the house that had burned, and the amount I'd have left from insurance after that. It wasn't much.

"But you'll still own the lot."

I frowned. "What good does that do me if I can't afford to rebuild on it?"

"It has value, and it will be yours free and clear once the insurance pays off the mortgage. We'll then be able to apply the value of the lot and its improvements, like sewer and water, to your new loan as a partial down payment." He tapped his chin with his pen, thinking. "You can't build a conventional house. But you might be able to swing a manufactured home."

"Oh, no. I'm not moving my family into one of them!"

He shrugged. "Suit yourself. But with the amount you'll have for a down payment, you could get yourself into a very nice house."

"But I want something that'll last."

He shrugged again. "Our loan department would give you a thirty year loan, Ms. Miller. We wouldn't do that if we didn't expect the houses to last at least that long." He fell silent, sensing my objections to a mobile home. Then he said, "It would cost you nothing to look."

It paid to talk to people and get new ideas. Suddenly, I blessed Melissa and the verbal kick in the rear she'd given me. A door opened that I'd never even seen before. I was still skeptical, but also realistic enough to realize I was rapidly running out of options.

I called Melissa from the bank and asked if she wanted to take the afternoon off and go house hunting with me. She picked me up fifteen minutes later, grinning, and complaining she knew all I wanted was a free ride.

"Of course." I grinned back, the first time I'd smiled in a week. "What else are you good for?"

She wanted to have lunch, but I insisted we drive straight to the only place in town that sold pre-fabs. Manufactured homes, I corrected myself mentally.

The salesman was like salesmen everywhere. He wanted to please. He showed us through several houses, each one beautiful. I was surprised by the quality of the workmanship. Any doubts I had about buying such a house evaporated.

The last house we looked at felt like home the instant I walked into it. Of course it had no upstairs like our old house had, but it was large, a four-bedroom ranch with a family room, two bathrooms, and even a beautiful fireplace in the living room. Surely I'd never be able to afford this!

"This line is being closed out, ma'am," the salesman said, as if reading my thoughts. "The manufacturer has marked down this floor plan four thousand dollars."

That helped, but it was still out of my budget by seven thousand dollars. Disappointed, I said, "Do you have anything similar? I love this house, but we're starting from nothing after the fire, and—"

"Oh, you're her?"

The fire had made the news, as had a few stories about our plight. Donations had poured in, but ours was a small town with major economic problems, so the donations hadn't amounted to all that much when it came to buying a house. The donations had all been earmarked for replacing other vital necessities. I'd counted on the insurance money to get us a new house.

"I'll be right back," the salesman said, leaving Melissa and I standing in the kitchen of the beautiful new house I knew I'd never own.

Discouraged, I flopped down on a nearby chair. "So close, and yet so far," I groused.

"We'll go to some other places. We'll find you something."

And to think, I'd actually started feeling alive again. Now I'd be back to waiting for someone to rescue me, like I had before.

"No," I said out loud.

"No, what?"

"I want this house. And I'm going to get it. Somehow."

The salesman returned. "I discussed it with my boss. We can lower the price by an additional four thousand dollars if you feel comfortable taking this house rather than ordering a new one. We need to get it off the lot in order to make room for next year's model."

"Yes!" Somehow, I'd scare up the extra money I needed. We might not get furniture for a few years, but we'd have the house! Elated, I went in to sign papers.

Seated at the salesman's desk, I suddenly wondered if I was doing the right thing after all. I could probably find a cheaper house somewhere else. Sure, it would be older and smaller, but we'd get by.

And suddenly, getting by wasn't good enough. With my newfound outlook, I decided to take the bull by the horns and really live for a change. I signed everything eagerly, up until the salesman asked me for the down payment.

"I don't have it. The insurance hasn't paid off yet."

"Okay. We'll just put this sale on hold for the time being and—"

"No." Last week I wouldn't have dared question someone like him. "I need that house now, the sooner the better. We want to be in by Thanksgiving."

"I'm sorry, Ms. Miller, but that's only possible with a substantial down payment."

I eyed him furiously. "How substantial?"

The figure he named would've made me cry, but that was in another life. The new, tough Darcy Miller did not cry, she got results. I whipped out the uncashed check I'd gotten for my ruined car. "This is all I have. Take it and I'll get the rest to you by the end of the week." How I'd accomplish that miracle I had no idea, but I felt sure I could. Satisfaction flooded through me as the man took my check after I'd signed it over to his business.

"Now, about delivery. I'd like the house installed next week, if possible." I had no idea what that involved, but I felt sure I could push to make it happen.

"I'm sorry, but there are no open delivery dates until after the first of the year. February fourth, in fact."

"That's unacceptable. We need a home now, right away."

"But other people are on the list ahead of you. I'm sorry."

I don't know where my courage came from. "Are those other people living in shelters?"

"No, I don't think so."

"Look, Mr. Jenkins, I'm not normally a pushy person, and as a rule, I wait my turn without complaint. But these are desperate circumstances for my family and me. Surely you can find some nice person willing to swap a delivery date with me so my children and I can have a house."

He muttered and mumbled but finally agreed. I felt like the most powerful person on earth as Melissa and I walked out of that office.

"Amazing. I'm truly impressed." Melissa's comment made me laugh. It felt good to laugh.

"Good. I hope you're impressed enough to give me a ride to work for the next six months, because that's probably how long it's going to take me to save up enough money to buy my own car."

She laughed. "No problem. I'm just glad to see you alive again."

That afternoon, Melissa and I brought Joy and Sam to see our new house. It didn't look nearly as nice as it had just that morning. The furniture, which hadn't been included in the cost of the home, had been removed and workmen were busy tearing plasterboard off the center wall so the two halves of the house could be separated for their short journey to our property. Still, my children were thrilled to see where they would be living. Each of them claimed a bedroom right away, dancing in the sunlight streaming in the windows. I hadn't realized till that moment how depressed my own mood had made them, how my worry and lethargy had affected them. It was good to see them smile again.

Mr. Jenkins met us as we were leaving. He'd talked to the bank, he said, and they'd given a verbal agreement to cover the loan until the paperwork and insurance were all straightened out. Stunned, I just stared, knowing banks didn't operate that way anymore. Then he assured us the house would be delivered and set up by the end of the next week, on Thanksgiving Day to be exact.

"But that's a holiday," I protested.

"I know. There is no other open date, so I discussed it with the crew. They all wanted to give up their holiday. Everyone in town's heard about the fire, you know. We've all wanted to help, but it's hard to know what to do sometimes. We talked about how we all had homes, and how you should have yours, too. It seemed appropriate for us to make that happen on Thanksgiving."

I hadn't cried, not really, since the fire. But Mr. Jenkins and his crew had really touched me. With tears streaming down my face, I marched right back into my new house and hugged each and every man there, Mr. Jenkins included. Most of them didn't say much, just various embarrassed noises, but I noticed all of them trying to be subtle as they wiped their eyes.

As I stood in the living room of my soon-to-be new home, I took stock once more of my life. I thought I'd lost everything. But as I hugged my kids and thought about the miracle that they and our beloved pets had survived, as I recalled Mr. Jenkins and his boss dropping the price of this beautiful house to put it in my price range, as I thought about the faith the banker had in me by covering my debts until the insurance paid off, as I looked around the room at the men who had volunteered to give up the holiday with their own families just to help a stranger, I realized I hadn't lost anything very important at all. And I knew our terrible fire had brought us the best Thanksgiving ever.

THE END

A FAMILY AFFAIR
This Was My Fantasy...Everyone Sitting Together And Enjoying Thanksgiving Dinner.

A million fantasies filled my head in the days following Colin's invitation to spend Thanksgiving with his children from his previous marriage, his parents, and him at his parents' home. My first thought was that we'd just moved our relationship up a level, something I'd wanted for months. By the time he picked me up on Wednesday I had visions of his going down on one knee, in front of his entire family, and asking me to marry him.

In my mind, this would be a Norman Rockwell Thanksgiving with lots of loving John-Boy Walton stuff tossed in. The drive to pick up his children, who lived in a mountainside chalet, would be romantic. Maybe there would even be a little snow. Not enough to cancel our trip, but a slight dusting, like sugar covering the ground.

Colin loaded my bags into his SUV, and then walked me to my side of the car to help me in. He kissed me and smiled. "Karen, I hope you know what you're getting into."

"Your car, for now," I quipped and gave him the best smile I could conjure.

"My kids can be little terrors when the mood strikes them. Hopefully Mom and Dad will make up for everything. They're absolutely going to love you."

"What makes you so sure?"

"Dad will like you because you're beautiful, and he appreciates a good-looking woman. Mom will like you because you're smart and compassionate. She studied nursing until she met Dad and decided to give it up in favor of marriage and a family. In her day, women didn't have to have it all."

"All that stuff is a myth," I said. "No one can have it all. Hurry up and let's get going. I'm dying to meet the children."

He gave me a look that I couldn't read at the time, but came to understand fully a few hours later.

Colin started the car and away we went. When he said that Gillian, his ex-wife, lived in the mountains, he wasn't kidding. The drive was long, through wooded areas that could barely accommodate one car on the road, much less two lanes.

We crossed an old wooden bridge over a fast-moving river, and turned right, going higher up the mountain until we reached a lovely wood and glass chalet. Colin said it had once been their summer home. Gillian was an illustrator for children's books and felt the mountain location gave her inspiration, so after the divorce she'd decided to live there.

"How do the kids get to school?" I asked.

"Gilly drives them to the foot of the mountain, where the mailbox is, and the school bus picks them up from there."

"It's so isolated."

"All the better to keep the kids out of trouble," he said.

We pulled to the side of the house. Colin stopped the car and hurried to let me out. "Colin, maybe I should wait in the car," I said.

"No, you should come in and meet the kids. Don't worry, Gillian doesn't bite. Even if she did, she'd never do it in front of her boy-toy. Her latest fling is spending the weekend with her. I think she said his name was Jeffrey. Frankly, I can't keep up with them." It was a relief to know that Colin's ex had someone in her life. I'd imagined her spending the long weekend alone, with no one to share her Thanksgiving dinner.

Arm in arm, we walked to the gorgeous wooden door that boasted stained glass windows. Colin rang the bell. Seconds later the door was opened by a tall, well-built, blond man who looked like a male model, and was holding a cup of something hot—I could see the steam rising from the drink.

"Come on in," the man said. "It's freezing out there."

"Thank you," Colin said. "Are the children packed and ready?"

"Gill is seeing to it now. How about some hot cider?"

Colin held my hand as we moved closer to the roaring fire. I gazed around the room, appreciating how beautifully it had been decorated. I wished he'd accept the offer of cider. It had been a very long drive—almost three hours, and we had slightly longer than that to go to get to his parents' house.

"We'll pass," Colin said. Oh, well.

"At least have a seat."

"We've been sitting for hours. Would you mind letting Gillian know that I'm here? We have a long drive ahead of us and I don't want to get in too late. My parents go to bed early. Then, she should know that. We were married for twelve years."

Colin sounded snappish, closing in on rude. If he had a problem with his ex, I didn't think he should take it out on the man who'd been nothing but polite since we'd arrived.

"I'll go let her know," the man said.

After he left, I turned to Colin and asked, "What's wrong with you? That man was as nice as could be and you acted like he had Ebola."

"Karen, drop it. None of this concerns you. It's between Gillian and me."

That was the first clue to let me know that perhaps Colin and I weren't as close as I'd hoped. He still had a foot in the world he'd shared with Gillian, and he wasn't over his divorce as much as he pretended to be. Then again, they did share two children.

From upstairs I heard a female voice. "I'm not ready to leave yet. My hair is still wet. Mom, tell him to hold his horses. It's bad enough that I have to spend the weekend with the Crypt Keepers."

"Ashley, you've known for a week that your father was coming to pick you up, and he'd be here by ten. It's ten-thirty. You've had plenty of time to get ready. Put a stocking hat on." This second female voice obviously belonged to Gillian.

"I'm not going out in the cold with a wet head," shouted Ashley. "Tell him to give me a half an hour. Make him a scotch. He always liked the stuff. Besides, Grant isn't packed either. Go hassle him, why don't you?"

I gazed at Colin, whose face was getting redder by the second. "So long John-Boy," I mumbled.

"What?" Colin asked.

"Nothing," I said. "Colin, it seems like we're going to be here a few minutes. Do you think I could use the restroom?"

"Under the stairs on the left-hand side," he said. "Don't take too long. We're going to be out of here in a couple of minutes if I have to drag the kids to the car. Gillian isn't going to get away with it this time."

It was then that I made a huge mistake. "From what I heard, she sounds like she's trying to make them get a move on. It isn't her fault."

Oh, the look he gave me. I was a traitor to the cause. Benedict Arnold probably got a lot of dirty looks, but I was convinced none were as damning as the look Colin gave me. His eyes were so narrow they were slits, and his jaw twitched. Forget about his mouth; it was a hard, straight line. Nothing showed of the lips that so often tenderly kissed me.

"Go to the bathroom, Karen. You don't know what you're talking about, and frankly, it's none of your business."

His harsh words made me wish I were back in my own apartment, curled up in bed with a novel and a cup of hot chocolate while Estelle, my cat, lay purring beside me. Unless I volunteered to work, that was how I spent my holidays. Both of my parents were dead, and my sister lived in Germany with her soldier husband and their little boy.

I went to the bathroom, did what I had to do, and hurried back to Colin. He was standing to the right of the fireplace, leaning against the wood-paneled wall, tapping his right foot.

"Fast enough?" I asked.

12

"They're still not ready," he said. "Karen, take the keys and get the SUV warmed up. I'll be out with Ashley and Grant in less than five minutes."

I went to the SUV and turned on the engine. It was freezing inside so I turned the heat as high as it would go. While I waited I heard the distant whine of emergency vehicles. Had I not been so miserable, I might have wondered what had happened. But I was miserable. So far, this had not been a Norman Rockwell painting. It was more like a really bad drama.

I'd never seen this side of Colin before. The man I knew was so different. I'd met Colin Douglas when he came to visit a friend of his at the hospital where I worked. He'd teased his friend about having such a pretty nurse. I lapped up the flattery like Estelle laps up cream.

Once it was established that I wasn't married, and he was equally single, Colin asked me to dinner. We had a blast; his sense of humor matched mine and we laughed constantly. Over the next few months we became closer, and I sensed that he felt the same way I did. I was in love.

I heard a door slam, and mingled voices all protesting and talking over one another. The trio cleared the side of the house, coming closer to the SUV. I turned off the engine and got out so Colin could drive.

"Karen, keep the engine running like I told you to," Colin snapped. "Ashley's hair is still wet, and Grant catches cold easily."

This was my introduction to Ashley and Grant Douglas. Colin tossed their things into the back, except for a bag that Grant held onto so tightly that his knuckles were white. Next the kids were strongly encouraged to get into the backseat and to buckle up.

"We've lost an entire hour," Colin said. "Nanna and Pa-paw are going to be worried."

"So call them," Ashley said.

"You know how the reception is in these mountains," Colin shot back.

"Go use Mom's phone."

"Ashley, just put your seatbelt on. I don't need to use your mother's phone or anything else that belongs to her."

"Oh, good grief," Ashley said. "Dad, if you're in such a hurry, I suggest you get your sweetie to move to the passenger seat unless you plan to drive sitting on her lap."

"Karen, you can move to your seat now," Colin said. "Just make sure we're in park."

I'd been driving for thirteen years, having started at fifteen when I got my permit. He didn't have to talk to me like a child. Of course I knew to keep the car in park. As much as I wanted to tell him so, I kept my mouth shut and moved to the passenger side, slamming my door to let Colin know I wasn't happy.

13

He pulled out of the driveway. Seconds later I heard Grant yell, "Damn!"

Without even looking back to see what was wrong, or to at least remind the boy that an eleven-year-old shouldn't use swear words, Colin shouted, "Put your game away, Grant, unless you can play it quietly."

"Sorry, Dad," the boy said.

We drove down the mountain. Light snow began to fall, but it wasn't like powdered sugar. It was wet slush. I held tightly to the armrest, wishing we were across the bridge. It hadn't seemed safe when it was dry. Crossing it when it was wet could send us sliding over the railing and into the river and certain death.

When we reached the turnoff that led to the bridge, I realized why I'd heard emergency sirens earlier. Cops, ambulances, and fire trucks were everywhere. Colin stopped and got out of the SUV. A few minutes later, he came back. His face was pale, and I knew something horrible had happened.

"There was an accident on the bridge. A car tried to pass a truck, got too close, the truck swerved and knocked down the guardrail. It jack-knifed and sent the car over the bridge. They haven't been able to find the car yet, and the bridge is closed to traffic until it can be repaired."

"So how do we get out of here?" I asked.

"We don't," Ashley said. "The only other way off the mountain is the back road, and it's so narrow that anything larger than a Volkswagen won't make it."

"Colin, what are we going to do?" I asked.

"Ashley, is the hotel in Braden still open? I know we can get there."

"Dad, Braden isn't even open. There's a food store and a hardware store. Everyone else closed down or went out of business. People go to Preston to shop. Unfortunately, they have to take the bridge to get there. Guess there won't be a lot of shoppers from here at the Super Wal-Mart Friday morning."

"There has to be some damn way off this mountain," Colin yelled.

"Screaming isn't going to get us out of here," I yelled back. "Colin, I'm tired of your attitude. Since we crossed the bridge on our way to pick up the kids you've been a total jerk. We should take the children back to their mother's house so they'll at least be warm, because if we keep the engine running, we're going to run out of gas and they'll have to walk back."

"Karen, I'll decide what to do with the children. I've told you before; they aren't any of your business."

14

"Dad, please listen to her," Ashley said. "It's snowing harder, and getting a ride back to the chalet won't be easy if you run out of gas."

"Colin, suck in your ego and do something," I said. "I didn't come on this trip to die of frostbite in the woods. Now you either turn this vehicle around and we go back to Gillian's, or I'm going to see if those rescue workers need a nurse."

"Do it, Daddy," Grant said. "I'm afraid of the woods. There are bears."

"Bears hibernate in the winter," Colin said.

"Frostbite doesn't," I said. "Look, I'm going to go help those workers. I'm not needed in this drama. If you don't care about the safety of your children, I'll see if I can get one of the policemen to take them home. Then you can freeze to death all by yourself."

"Karen, I've never seen this side of you," Colin said.

A smart remark tickled my tongue, but I kept it back in case I needed it later. Instead, I got out of the SUV and ran to one of the ambulances. "My name is Karen Wells. I'm an emergency room nurse. Can I be of any help here?"

"Thanks, Ms. Wells, but it's covered. They were able to get the truck driver out of the truck and get him into a bus on the other side of the river. He's already at the hospital in Preston. We're just hanging around in case one of the rescue workers needs us."

"Is there a hospital on this side of the river?"

"Nope. We have a firehouse and my ambulance service, as well as a small police station. With the bridge damaged, and no immediate way to move the truck, even if we had an emergency we wouldn't be able to get anyone to the hospital. There used to be another road, but a few years ago an avalanche trashed it. To get out of here you'd have to take the road on the opposite side, and it's not much more than a bike trail."

"So anyone on this side is stuck?"

He gave me a nod and a fast salute.

"There are two children in the red SUV who live up on the mountain. I'm with their father, and he refuses to take them home. Do you know of anyone who would drive them?"

"If you're talking about the Douglas kids, I think Bobby Joseph would be glad to give them a ride. His wife is a friend of their mother's. I'll ask him if you want me to. He's just sitting around in his cop car watching the divers."

"Thank you," I said and walked back to Colin's SUV. I opened the passenger side door. "For now there isn't anything I can do to help the rescue workers, but I have arranged for you kids to get a ride home. And I think I'll go with you."

Without waiting for Colin to speak, the children gathered their things and hurried out of the vehicle. I got my bags and joined them.

What was going through Colin's mind was taking a long time to formalize.

"Why don't you come back with us?" I asked. "You could at least call your parents to tell them we won't be there."

"We'll be there. It's just going to be later than I anticipated."

"Colin, it's sleeting. The bridge is badly damaged, and a truck is stuck on it. A big truck that will take time to be towed off. And unless the truck is taken off, no one can work on the bridge. It could be days."

"I never thought you would be the sort of woman who'd betray a man," he said. "Especially a man who loves you as much as I do."

"If you really love me then come with me. Better still, let's drive back to the chalet with the children. What must they be thinking?"

"I know what they're thinking. They'll get to be at home with their mother instead of spending the holiday with me. They never want to spend the holidays with me. Every year it's the same thing. Something always happens so they don't have to be with me over Thanksgiving or Christmas."

"This year is different, darling. They're going to be with you. Heck, they might even be with you until New Years, because the way the ambulance driver talked, it's not going to be an easy task fixing the bridge."

"Fine, you win. We'll go to Gillian's together."

I told the kids to put their things back into the SUV. Their father was going with us. Both looked happy, which surprised me. Had Colin been right? Did the children resent him so much that they didn't want to spend holidays with him? Why, I wondered, would that be?

We drove back up the mountain, slipping once in a while on the wet road. The drive was quiet. Only the occasional sound of Grant's video game broke the silence. As soon as Colin parked the car, both children grabbed their belongings and ran to the house. When Colin and I reached the front door, the attractive man who'd greeted us before was standing there, wearing nothing but silk boxers and an embarrassed look on his face.

In front of the fire, wrapped in a faux bearskin rug, was a woman, whom I presumed was Gillian. We hadn't met earlier. I didn't see the children anywhere.

"Wonderful," Colin said. "You couldn't wait until they were gone an hour before you hit the sheets with your boyfriend."

"It's a rug, Colin. Not a sheet. And why shouldn't Jeffrey and I enjoy some intimacy? We're the ones who have to be careful around the kids all the time while you and your girlfriend can roll around in bed whenever it suits you."

I held out my hand to Jeffrey. "I'm Karen Wells," I said.

He shook my hand. "Jeffrey Warner."

16

"Nice to meet you. I apologize for bursting in on you both, but the bridge was out and we really had no choice. Colin and I will check on the children to make sure they didn't leave anything."

I grabbed Colin's sleeve and tugged. Together we went up the staircase. I heard Ashley talking on the phone. "Oh, Trevor, it was so frightening. If we had to walk back we would have died of frostbite. Daddy's girlfriend is a nurse and she said we faced certain death."

Glancing up at Colin, I smiled. "There's the reason Ashley didn't want to leave. She has a boyfriend."

"Ashley is barely fourteen," he said.

"Fourteen with a crush. A combination that makes for high drama."

From Grant's room came the sound of all-out warfare. "I'll get you this time, Lord Vader," Grant said. I peered into his room and saw him stretched out on the floor, holding the controls to a game system that was playing out its carnage on a flat-screen television.

"Do you have one of those game devices at your parents'?" I asked Colin. "I know you don't have one at your apartment."

"My parents are so old fashioned they don't even have cable."

"Then I suspect we've found the reason Grant likes staying at home."

"Of course. Gillian buys them all this stuff to bribe them so they won't want to be with me. And I'll bet you she set up the tryst between Ashley and that boy."

"How would she have the time?" I asked. "Between Jeffrey and causing global warming?"

"Karen, I don't appreciate your sarcastic side."

"And I don't enjoy your neurotic side. Colin, we're stuck here, and if you behave we might get to stay inside, where it is warm. Otherwise Gillian might have Jeffrey toss us out on our ears."

"Colin," Gillian called. "Come down here."

We walked down the stairs. She'd put on slacks and a sweater. Jeffrey had on the same jeans and flannel shirt he'd worn earlier. It was apparent that he was younger than she was, but it wasn't a drawback because Gillian was a beautiful woman. Her body was trim and shapely, and her skin still had a glow that younger women would have envied. I'll confess I wished I looked half as good, and I was younger than she was by at least ten years.

"Now what is this all about?" she asked.

"There was a terrible wreck on the bridge. A delivery truck and a car tried to cross at the same time. The car went off the bridge into the river. The truck is still on the bridge, though the cab is straddling the guardrails. No one can get over it."

"Too bad you decided to buy a gas guzzler. If you had a car like

17

mine you could get down using the other road."

"What I drive is none of your business, Gillian," Colin snapped.

"When everyone is starving because of all the damage you've done to this planet it will be everyone's business."

"Oh, don't give me that crap. I had to listen to the Green House Effect for the first six years of our marriage, and global warming for the last six. Gilly, you seem to have the idea that I alone am going to trash the planet. Babe, read a real book sometime. One volcano does more damage to the atmosphere than all the SUVs in this country."

"What will you do when we run out of fuel?" she asked. "Where will you put your SUV then?"

"How about I shove it up your—"

"Colin!" I screamed. "Honey, your children are upstairs and I'm sure they can hear you."

"Oh, let him rant, Karen. By the way, I'm Gillian. Call me Gill if you like, but please, do not ever call me Gilly."

"Would anyone like some cider?" Jeffrey asked.

"I would love some," I answered. "I'll even help you fix it." More than anything, I wanted out of the same room with Colin and Gillian.

Jeffrey led me to the kitchen where he then took a jug of cider from the refrigerator. "I'm sorry about all of this," I said.

"Not your fault," he said. "They can't be in the same room without fighting. You should hear their phone calls. I feel sorry for the kids. Gill yells profanity at Colin. God only knows what he says to her. The kids are a wreck after every phone call."

"Why does she even talk to him?"

"She's still angry about the divorce. So is he. I've started answering the phone so that when he calls he only talks to Grant and Ashley."

"Am I rude to ask how long you've been together?"

"I met Gill at a gallery opening two years ago. She invited me to visit here and one thing led to another. We're both artists, though I'm into abstracts and she's an illustrator."

"Would I have seen your work?" I was really asking if he was successful, or just a kept man with a desire to become famous.

"I would hope so," he said. "My last gallery showing completely sold out, and I'm currently doing a new collection that has already sold."

"You're successful," I said.

"More than Gill, and more than Colin. I'm not a kept man, Karen. I love Gill. Someday I'd like to marry her, but I don't see that day coming anytime soon."

He finished warming the cider and poured it into four cups, then stirred it with a stick of cinnamon. "Let me get the doors," I said. Together we went into the great-room. Jeffrey put the tray on a table. He served Gillian first.

"Is there anything to put in this?" Colin asked.

"There is rum and scotch in the cabinet beneath the Monet," Jeffrey said.

"Beneath the Monet," Colin said with a smirk. "Jeffrey, I do know which painting the Monet is. I gave it to Gilly on our fifth anniversary."

"She told me. That's why I knew you'd know where I was talking about."

Colin went and got the scotch. He poured some into his cider. He drank a long drink and poured more. "Anyone else want to kick their cider up a notch?"

All declined. If there was an opportunity to get out of the chalet and back to civilization, I wasn't going to be too drunk to grab it. "Colin, we should call your parents," I said.

"Yes, Colin, do call Francis and Boyd," Gillian said. "If you wait much longer, they'll be passed out and won't hear the phone."

"Don't start on my parents," Colin snapped. "They helped us plenty when we were first married, unlike your family. Mom and Dad gave us a roof over our heads until I found a decent job after I was laid off from Petrie and Holmes."

"I'd have rather been homeless," Gillian snapped back. "Francis had something to say about everything I did. She practically took Ashley away from me because she thought she was a better mother."

"Mom was only trying to help you. Gillian, you were so wrapped up in your art classes that you barely knew Ashley was alive."

"I knew she was alive; I was the one who took care of her every night after Francis passed out. The reason I took my art classes so early was so I'd be home before she started drinking."

"You're calling my mother a drunk? How about your own mother? Constance never met a drug she didn't like. Tell me, Gilly, does she still take four different anti-depressants each day, along with all those other pills that she swears are keeping her alive?"

"My mother has never enjoyed good health."

"Stop it," I screamed. "This is wrong. And I don't care if Mr. and Mrs. Douglas drink or not, they deserve the courtesy of a phone call. If you won't call them, Colin, give me the number and I will."

Ashley walked down the stairs. "It's okay, Karen. I called them because I knew Mom and Dad would get into a fight and forget. When they fight they forget everything and everybody. I also called the police station and they said it would be four days before the bridge can be repaired. Tomorrow is Thanksgiving and they can't get anyone to work on it. Besides, they have to get supplies in and that's not going to be easy."

19

"Why?" Colin asked.

"It's sleeting, and they say the roads might ice over. Mom, I told Trevor he could come over later. That's okay, isn't it?"

"How is he going to get here?" Colin asked.

"Dad, I'm smart enough to pick a boyfriend who lives on this side of the bridge. His house is about ten minutes away. He's sixteen and has a jeep."

Gillian crossed the room to Ashley and smiled. "Of course Trevor can come. We'll be happy to have him."

"Okay. And don't worry. I've already told him about how much you fight. He doesn't care. But Dad, please don't get too drunk. You talk crazy when you get drunk. I'd like Trevor's first impression of you to be a good one."

In all the months I'd been involved with Colin, I'd never seen him lose control. He would have a cocktail when we went to dinner and share a bottle of wine with me sometimes, but he never acted strangely. If anything, he was more cheerful.

"Ashley, honey, I would never do anything to embarrass you or your brother," Colin said. "I love you both and want you to be happy."

"We love you too, Daddy," she said. "And we want you to be happy, so please don't fight with Mom."

"You'd might as well tell him to fly off this mountain," Gillian said.

"Mom, you're as bad as he is. Even when he's nice to you, you always find something to throw up to him. All of us have seen how you act when you're together."

The girl was right. We'd all seen the wrath of the exes. I'd known divorced couples that still carried a grudge. The difference was, I'd never seen them throw barbs at each other the way that Colin and Gillian did.

Jeffrey, who had gone for cider refills, came back into the room. Colin added scotch to his, just as he had before. "It's only a little," he said to Ashley. "Something to warm up my old bones."

Ashley shook her head and ran up the stairs. I slumped down on a big, puffy brown chair and sipped my cider.

"We should make sleeping arrangements," Jeffrey said. "I would be happy to sleep in the den and give my room to Colin and Karen."

Colin smirked. "I'm sure Karen wouldn't be comfortable sleeping with Gillian and me."

"Jeffrey and I don't share a bedroom, Colin. We're much more discreet than that around the children."

"And so should we be," I said. "I noticed that Ashley has twin beds in her room. Maybe she will let me use one of them, and Colin can take the den. There is no reason for Jeffrey to be inconvenienced in his own home."

"His home?" Colin said. "Just where did you get the idea this was his home?"

"He lives here, Colin, and I'm sure he carries his own weight," I said.

"Exactly what were you two talking about for so long in the kitchen?" Colin asked.

"Art," I said. "Colin, Jeffrey is a successful artist."

"Well, I don't agree with the sleeping arrangements," Colin said. "After all, I was the one who bought this place, and I spent every spare dime and minute fixing it up the way she wanted it." He gestured toward Gillian.

She began laughing. It was a nasty laugh, worthy of Bette Davis in one of those over-the-top black and white dramas they showed on A&E. "You pinched pennies so tightly, I thought you'd die of copper poison."

"Which you would have loved. Then you would have gotten all of my insurance."

Dark had crept up on us as quietly as Estelle stalked a mouse. Time doesn't just fly when you're having fun. Other than me, the only person to notice was Jeffrey. "I should start dinner," he said. "How's lasagna?"

"I love it," I said. "And so does Colin."

Gillian shot me a look that made me feel like the intruder that I was. She turned away and followed Jeffrey into the kitchen. Colin poured more scotch into his cup and sat on the footrest in front of the puffy chair.

"I'm so sorry to have dragged you into this," he said. "It's not the weekend I had planned."

"If you're really sorry, please stop fighting with Gillian. Colin, it doesn't accomplish anything."

"Karen, you have no idea what that woman did to me. I've tried to keep my family out of our relationship."

"She's not your family anymore, Colin. Whatever she did to you is over. Nothing can change it. Please, for me, let's eat dinner, meet Ashley's boyfriend, and find a reason to go to bed early. Tomorrow there might be a way that we can leave here; perhaps there is a bed and breakfast somewhere close by and we can go to it."

He put his arms around me and pulled me into his embrace. We held each other, hugging for a long time. I felt as though I had rediscovered the Colin that I knew and loved. At most it would be a few days, and then we would find a way to get back to the city, where our lives were sane and sweet.

Gillian and Jeffrey set a very nice table. They opened two bottles of good red wine, and the aroma of the lasagna was intoxicating. I

21

hadn't eaten a bite since early that morning, and then it had only been a plain bagel with a cup of black coffee.

"This looks and smells wonderful," I said.

"We've set up dinner for the children in the breakfast room," Jeffrey said. "Hopefully we'll have a relaxing dinner. I'm sure you could use some peace and quiet, Karen."

We took our seats. Jeffrey served the lasagna, and Gillian passed around warm, crusty garlic bread. After our plates were set, Jeffrey poured the wine, setting the bottles on the table in easy reach.

The lasagna was different from any I'd ever had before, but it was tasty. Unfortunately, it didn't sit well with Colin. "What's this green, leafy stuff?" he asked.

"Spinach," Gillian said.

"There isn't any meat," Colin pointed out.

"It's vegetarian lasagna," she said. "For the love of God, Colin, just eat it or don't eat it. Frankly, I don't care. There's cheese in the fridge. Make a sandwich if you don't like the lasagna."

"I should have known you'd become a vegetarian," Colin said. "You've always been depressed because you were born too late to be a hippie. Twenty bucks says you have some marijuana stashed in your dresser drawer."

"Oh, go to hell," she screamed and tossed her wine in Colin's face. Gillian ran from the table up the stairs. Jeffrey handed Colin a napkin and chased after her.

"So much for peace and quiet," I said. "Couldn't you have just eaten the cheese and noodles and kept your mouth shut?"

"I send that woman plenty of money every month so that my children will have the things they need, and now I find out that they aren't even being fed meat? Karen, you're young, and you don't have kids, so you can't understand this."

"I'm a nurse, and I see plenty of vegetarians. Most are as healthy as anyone else. They find ways to substitute meat."

"I'll bet he's the one who started this. He can't be much older than you are. He's probably into all that New Age stuff, and my kids are suffering for it."

Given a choice, I'd have dumped a bottle of the excellent wine on Colin. Instead, I reconsidered and decided to drink it. I ate and fixed myself a second helping, which I also polished off, all the while sipping the wine.

Jeffrey returned. He carried the food into the kitchen, and then came out with a large tray, stopping for a second to grab the second bottle of wine. "We'll have dinner in Gill's room," he said.

"I'll clean up the kitchen," I offered.

"Karen, no offence, but I think it would be best if you watch a movie in the den. You and Colin will have privacy there. Ashley said you're welcome to use her second bed. I will see you in the morning."

He left us. Colin stood and stared at Jeffrey as he carried the tray up the stairs. The look on his face was dark and threatening.

"I'll just bet they're having dinner in her room. They're probably going to finish what they started before we showed up."

"So what? They've been together for two years. He loves her, and he has his own money, so he's not after hers. Colin, you act like a jealous lover instead of an ex-husband."

It was at that moment that I got it.

Colin and Gillian hadn't moved on because they were still in love with each other. There was no reason for her not to marry Jeffrey; and I thought that Colin wanted to marry me eventually. The truth was, Gillian and Colin would rather fight with each other than love anyone else.

"I think I'll pass on the movie. I'm tired, Colin. I want a shower and then bed. See you in the morning."

Just as I reached the stairs, the doorbell rang. Because I was closest, I opened the door. A lanky boy with red hair and freckles, wearing a heavy jacket, a wool scarf, and a knit cap stood shaking in the cold.

"You must be Trevor," I said.

"Yes, ma'am. And I'll bet you're Karen."

I smiled and nodded. "Come in out of the cold. Warm up by the fire. I'll tell Ashley you're here."

As I left the room, I heard Colin talking to Trevor. Hopefully he wouldn't make an ass of himself. Ashley deserved better than that. After telling her that Trevor was there, I told her I was going to bed.

"Don't wait up for me," she said, giggling like the schoolgirl that she was. Ashley showed me the back stairs. I made my escape without another drama to deal with.

That night I slept fitfully, wishing I were home, or even at the hospital. The next day was Thanksgiving, and I'd rather eat a hospital turkey dinner with the emergency room staff than have to sit down to a meal surrounded by controversy.

Morning came, and I noticed that Ashley's bed hadn't been slept in. Across the hall, from Grant's room, I heard someone crying. I knocked on the door and Grant opened it. His little face was streaked with tears. Sitting on his bed was Ashley, and her eyes were swollen and red too.

"What happened?" I asked.

"Mom and Dad got into it while Trevor was here," Ashley said. "We had gone for a ride to have some time alone. When we came back Dad was waiting for me and he was furious because I'd left the house.

23

He'd had too much to drink and started grilling Trevor. He accused him of being a sex maniac. Mom told Dad to go to bed. Then they got into a terrible fight. Dad said that Mom didn't care who I went out with as long as I didn't disrupt her time with Jeffrey."

"Oh, I'm so sorry," I said.

"Karen, it got really bad. Mom told Dad that if anyone was a sex maniac it was him. He was the one who always wanted to have sex, and he didn't care if he used protection or not. Then he told her that he wouldn't have married her if she'd been bright enough to use birth control. Jeffrey stepped in and tried to make it stop. Dad took a swing at him. Then Jeffrey floored Dad and knocked him out. They put him in the den to sleep it off. But I don't care. I'm the reason Mom and Dad got married and had horrible lives. If she hadn't gotten pregnant, she'd have never married him. I heard her say so. And he wouldn't have married her."

I put my arms around the girl and held her while she sobbed. Grant, who obviously cared a lot about his sister—almost as much as he cared about video games—joined me in comforting her.

There was a knock on the door. I prayed that it wasn't Colin. My prayer was answered. Jeffrey stood there, looking like he'd just been through the worst night of his life, which he probably had.

"I have breakfast made. The road is still closed. Unfortunately, Karen, you and Colin will have to stay here a bit longer. I've arranged for Thanksgiving dinner to be brought in for you and Colin."

"Please don't go to any trouble for us," I said.

"Gill has asked me to divide the house while you are here. You will have use of the breakfast room and the den. And you may use the extra bed in Ashley's room. But under no circumstances are you and Colin to come into any other part of the house."

"She didn't do anything," Ashley said. "If it hadn't been for Karen, Dad would have let us freeze yesterday."

Jeffrey sat on the bed and put his hand on my shoulder. "Karen, I do apologize to you. Ashley is right. You have been gracious and kind, but you are Colin's guest, not ours, so you will have to obey the ground rules. Also, there will be no drinking."

"Sounds fair to me," I said. "I'll come down for breakfast in a couple of minutes."

Grant left with Jeffrey, and I sat with Ashley. She told me all about Trevor, and insisted that they'd never had sex. They liked to drive out to an old ski lift that had closed more than thirty years before and watch the stars. Like teenagers everywhere, they shared their hopes and dreams, as well as their sorrows.

Soon we went to breakfast. Ashley decided to eat in the breakfast room with her father and me. Colin was filled with apologies, which came with a dozen justifications. All of them pointed to Gillian as the culprit.

Ashley held her head down, watching her food grow cold, unable to eat while Colin continued to overly explain everything. A loud crash from the kitchen stopped his diatribe.

"You bastard," Gillian screamed and came running into the breakfast room. She raised her hand and slapped Colin. "Since we filed for divorce you've done nothing but put me down to our children. For the last four years all they ever hear from you is what a witch I am. Is it any wonder they don't want to spend time with you?"

"They deserve to know the truth," Colin said. "And I'm sure you tell them about all of my faults."

"Stop it," I screamed. "You people are driving me crazy. And you're driving your children crazy. Someday they'll grow up and won't want to see either one of you. They'll move as far away from you as possible, and they'll always have an excuse not to come home for holidays."

"What do you know about it?" Gillian said to me.

"Plenty. My parents have been dead for six years, but before they died, while my sister and I were growing up, they made our lives hell with their arguing. We never had a nice Christmas or Thanksgiving. Every holiday ended the same. Yelling, cursing, breaking things. Savannah eloped before she finished high school. She married a guy in the Army and never came home for holidays. As soon as I graduated, I got a job and worked my way through nursing school."

"You never told me that," Colin said.

"And you never told me that you were still in love with your ex-wife," I said.

They both gave me incredulous looks. My comment left the room silent. Even Jeffrey stared at me.

"Why did you divorce him, Gillian?" I asked.

"Because he was a control freak who wouldn't try new things and didn't want me to try them either. It was like he had to keep me under his nose all of the time. Once I had a great job offer, but Colin made me turn it down and keep working from home. He said it was for the sake of the kids; his mother never worked once he was born."

"Colin, why did you divorce Gillian?" I asked.

"She was a witch. Nothing was ever enough for her. I provided a nice apartment for us in the city, and I bought this place to make her happy, but nothing pleased her. She changed her mind constantly, always wanting to take on some crazy new project."

"Did either of you cheat on the other?"

"No," they said in unison.

"Look, I don't care to discuss this with you," Gillian said. "If I wanted Dr. Phil, I'd have invited him to Thanksgiving dinner."

"Sorry, but after all the crap you've subjected us to in the last twenty-four hours, I think I have the right to know where I stand. I thought Colin was in love with me and that we had a future, but I see that we don't. I'm not you, Gillian, and I never will be. I don't cruise with the butterflies. I'm the lady who tries to soothe a family when there has been a crisis. Guess that's what I'm trying to do now. It's a lot easier when your tools are needles and sutures."

Jeffrey looked stricken. I was like the child who exposed the naked emperor. I'd put into words something he'd felt for a long time, and now that the words were out, they could no longer be ignored.

"You do still love him," Jeffrey said to Gillian. "That's why you have so many rules about how we conduct ourselves. I've asked you to marry me so many times, but you don't want to. You're still in love with Colin. All I am is someone to keep you company and join in your adventures."

The phone rang. I prayed that it would be news that there was a way off the mountain. It was Trevor. Ashley took the call in her bedroom. Grant had already barricaded himself in his room.

"Karen, you know I love you," Colin said. "You're everything I've ever wanted in a woman."

"I'm everything your mother has ever wanted you to have in a woman, not what you wanted, or you wouldn't have fallen in love with Gillian in the first place."

Jeffrey had quietly begun clearing the table. He retreated into the kitchen. I followed him. On the butcher-block table sat the food he'd begun preparing for Thanksgiving. I walked toward it and breathed in the aromas that would only improve when cooked.

"It wasn't my idea," he said.

"What wasn't?"

"She wanted to become a vegetarian and got all of these books on it and we learned to alter some of our favorite recipes. Actually, it was fun. Then, Gill has always been fun, always ready to try new things. A few months ago she became interested in Kabala and bought these red strings for us to wear. That was as far as it went, though. Gill doesn't stick with things long. She just wants to know about them."

"You really love her."

"And you really love him. I can tell. The problem is, they both love conflict. It was the driving passion in their lives. Once she told me that after they fought, they always had the best sex. Guess I should have fought with her instead of trying to make her happy."

"Jeffrey, they'll never get back together. After Colin leaves here, I doubt if you'll even see him again until time for the kids to visit. Maybe it would be best if you brought the kids to him."

He winced. "I suggested it once. She wouldn't hear of it. She said

26

if he wanted them, he'd damn well come pick them up. Now I know why. She wanted to see him, even if they argued. You won't believe how weird she's been this past week after she found out you were going to dinner at his folks' house. She has ranted and raved, saying the two of you were going to corrupt the kids' morals."

"Sounds like jealousy to me," I said. "Jeffrey, have you made a dessert yet? The wife of one of my patients was a vegetarian, and she gave me the best recipe for dairy-free chocolate pie."

"We're not strict vegan; dairy isn't a problem."

"Is there anything else I can do?"

"Get me off this mountain."

"I wish I could. We'd both leave."

The day moved on. I helped Jeffrey in the kitchen as much as possible. Colin and Gillian continued to argue. Ashley stayed in her room, and so did Grant. Around two, Jeffrey and I put the food on the table in the dining room. I fixed two plates for Colin and me and took them to the breakfast room.

When we tried to find Gillian and Colin to tell them that dinner was ready, they were nowhere in the house. Jeffrey looked outside and saw that Gillian's VW was gone. "Damn, dinner isn't going to be worth eating," Jeffrey said.

I felt sorry for him. He'd gone to so much trouble. Give him credit; the man had made a turkey out of sweet potatoes. It was cute, and something only a true artist could pull off. An hour passed. Jeffrey decided that since Gillian had changed the rules, he could as well.

"Karen, you're a nice lady, and you don't deserve to be put at the kiddies table. I'm going to get dinner on the table in the dining room; call the kids and tell them we're going to eat."

I got the children and we went to the table. Jeffrey had re-heated the food. We helped ourselves and were about to eat when the front door opened. Gillian entered first; she was wrapped in a heavy cape. Colin followed her.

There are things about a person that only his lover would recognize. I knew the look on Colin's face after he'd had sex. And Jeffrey must have known Gillian equally well. He stood, his face showing deep hurt. I'm sure mine was the same, because it was obvious to Jeffrey and to me that they had just had sex.

I saw Jeffrey grab the tablecloth. Seconds later, china and silver flew across the dining room. He'd pulled the tablecloth from the table the way I'd seen magicians do it; only Jeffrey hadn't left the plates and glasses on the table. They were shattered on the hardwood floor. Food splattered the walls.

"You bitch," he screamed. "All these years I've done everything I could to make you happy."

Ashley and Grant were crying. I took their hands and led them upstairs. Colin and I would talk later. For now, I just wanted to be out of the room. Once again, a family Thanksgiving had turned into hell on earth.

Up in Ashley's room, the children cried. I cried, too, but it wasn't just because of Colin. So many memories flooded my head, breaking my fragile heart all over again. The grownups had once again destroyed the day, leaving no reason to be joyous or thankful.

"Don't cry, Karen," Ashley said. "I don't know why Jeffrey got so mad, he doesn't act like that. I'm sure he's sorry."

"It's not Jeffrey, Ashley. I'm crying because I remember other times when people were cruel to each other and they ruined holidays. Just once I'd like to sit down at a family dinner table on Thanksgiving and enjoy the meal and the company."

"That's not a problem," she said. "But we'll have to sneak out. I'll leave a note so they won't worry about us."

"What are you talking about?"

"Look, Grant and I would like to have a nice Thanksgiving, too. I happen to know where we can have one. Just let me make a quick phone call."

I assumed there was a diner that we could go to, but I was wrong, and never so happy to be wrong. After the call, Ashley told me to get my coat. She and Grant bundled up in theirs, and we crept down the back stairs and out of the house. We walked to the edge of the road and waited behind some trees.

Cold wind blew against us, so we clung together to stay warm. A few minutes later, I heard the sound of a car. It was Trevor in his jeep. When he stopped, Grant and I got into the backseat and Ashley got up front with him.

"You sure your mom doesn't mind?" Ashley asked.

"She's happy to have more people so we won't have to eat turkey all next week," he said.

We rode to a large farmhouse. When we went to the door, we were greeted by Trevor's parents, and a host of aunts, uncles, and cousins, along with Trevor's four brothers and three sisters.

The table was enormous and loaded down with food, and the turkey hadn't been made out of sweet potatoes. Before dinner, the family joined hands and thanked God for their blessings, which were each other.

This was my fantasy; a loving family enjoying God's bounty. No one cursed or belittled anyone. They laughed and shared stories of their adventures over the past year. They made me feel as though I belonged.

In the three hours I spent with Trevor's family, I forgot about the fact that the man I was in love with had cheated on me with his ex-wife, and that I was stuck in a hell house with people who only lived to make each other miserable. Instead, I let myself relax and be happy.

"Want to stay and play cards?" Trevor's mother, Margaret, said.

"I think we'd better go back," I said. "They might have decided to call the police and report us missing."

"It's been lovely meeting you, Karen. Thanks for the advice on treating my headaches. I'm going to give it a try."

"You're very welcome," I said. As we left we called our goodbyes. Goodbye Margaret, goodbye Uncle Frank, goodbye Sarah Lynn. It was a Walton moment if there ever was one. I only wished someone had been named John-Boy.

On the ride back Trevor told me that he would be happy to take me down the mountain in his jeep. He'd made the run a few times and it wasn't a problem. The sleet had stopped, and the sun had melted the icy spots. I agreed, and we arranged for him to pick me up the next day. I'd go into Preston and take a train back to the city.

That night Colin tried to talk to me, but I had nothing to say to him. Jeffrey had left Gillian, taking her VW as a means of escape. Colin would take her to pick it up after the bridge was fixed.

Early, while everyone slept except Ashley and me, I packed, bundled up, and we went together to meet Trevor. She was along to keep him company. In Preston I bought a ticket and boarded the commuter train. Surprised, I found Jeffrey on the same train.

"I thought you left last night," I said.

"Had to wait until today. Nothing was running when I got here so I stayed in the hotel."

"Well, at least we're out of the chaos," I said.

"He wants you back," Jeffrey said. "At least that's what he said. And she didn't want me to leave."

"Do you believe them?"

"I want to."

Though we sat together, there was practically no conversation on the ride to the city. I grabbed the first cab I could and went home, where I immediately grabbed Estelle and went to bed for a really good cry.

Colin called me on Monday and wanted to talk. I told him it wasn't necessary. Whatever there was between us didn't exist anymore. I'll confess that it hurt to shut him out of my life, but I wanted something different. What I wanted wasn't a fairytale, because I'd seen it for myself.

I wanted a life of happy Thanksgivings with a family that loved and respected each other. I wanted the life I'd witnessed at Trevor's house—a real Walton family that took joy in being together.

THE END

THANKSGIVING DANCE
The Start Of A Holiday Tradition.

Annoyed that I had to park so far from the supermarket, I hurried across the parking lot, turning my coat collar up against the blustery November wind. Dried leaves skittered across my ankles as I strode. It was two days before Thanksgiving, and the supermarket lot was jammed with cars. I could see through the store's large windows that long lines awaited in checkout.

I pulled my collar closer, angry at letting myself run out of cat food, and irritated that Heather West's mother decided to show up at school unannounced as I was going out on my lunch break to buy the cat food. Frantic that her fifth grader was failing math, Mrs. West didn't want to wait till after the holiday to discuss the problem with me. But I loved teaching and made sure I was always available to my students' parents, even when the discussion kept me from lunch. My stomach rumbled now, reminding me I'd only eaten an English muffin and an apple all day.

My high heels clacked on the hard surface as I dodged a runaway shopping cart and cars driving too fast looking for available spots. Holidays sometimes brought out the worst in people, the stress making them careless.

Thanksgiving.

Regret jolted through me. My favorite holiday would be forever tainted by sorrow. Two years ago at this time, I was preparing for my Thanksgiving wedding. A day later my fiancé was dead. The unfairness of it all roiled my stomach. Anger and grief were my constant companions now, freezing my heart.

In the years Dane had been dead, I'd been unable to cry. I tried, Lord knows I tried, but the tears wouldn't come. They were in me, seething to get out, but my anger held them tight inside.

Distracted by my melancholy thoughts, I stumbled on the uneven ground just as another runaway cart veered toward me. Someone grabbed my arm, pulling me out of the charging cart's way. A strong hand, steadying and sure, held me.

"Are you okay?" The deep male voice, rich as melted chocolate, soothed my jangled nerves.

I looked up. My gaze locked with aquamarine eyes, the color of the Caribbean in the honeymoon brochures I still kept in my dresser at home. At the thought of my honeymoon, regret and guilt formed a knot in my chest. Regret that Dane, my best friend since high school and the man I'd planned to marry, was dead. And guilt—because when I looked into this stranger's eyes, that part of me that had died with Dane came alive as sensual awareness coursed through me.

Fighting my response to the man who held me, I reluctantly pulled free. "I'm fine now. Thanks for helping."

He smiled, white teeth flashing in a tanned face, and I forgot to breathe. Exquisite, flashed in my mind. I scanned his face and took in his rugged features: sharply chiseled cheekbones, a strong, high-bridged nose, full lips. Masculine and powerful. Just being near him made my legs weaken. I clenched my glove-clad hands at my sides—afraid I'd reach out and run my fingers through his thick curly black hair.

He frowned and cupped my elbow. Concern shone from his amazing eyes. "Are you sure you're okay?"

My face heated in embarrassment; I could only nod. A car horn honked loudly nearby, and I jumped.

"We'd better get out of the way," he said. Gripping my elbow, he helped guide me across the parking lot to the store entrance.

We stood just outside the automatic doors and stared at each other as shoppers, carts laden, moved around us. He released my arm, and I missed his reassuring touch.

"Thanks again," I said.

"No problem." He smiled that devastating smile of his. My pulse jumped.

"If you're sure you're okay. . ." he said.

"I'm fine."

"All right then, I'll get my groceries and be on my way."

In the area where I'd almost fallen, he gestured to a cart filled with groceries.

"Oh, you left your cart to help me," I said. "Please don't let me hold you up any longer."

He gave me a lingering look, then turned and strode toward his cart.

My insides quivering, I watched him walk away. Long legs encased in jeans and a leather jacket covering wide shoulders, he looked like every woman's romance fantasy.

Guilt overtook me, and I shrugged aside my dangerous thoughts. I was still mourning Dane. His death had killed my heart and my feelings. I wasn't supposed to notice other men, much less feel sexual stirrings. I had to remain loyal to Dane.

Someone jostled me from behind, and I hurried into the store, but thoughts of the handsome stranger followed me. I'd never seen him before, and yet he provoked something hot and aching deep inside me. I decided it was just my imagination, brought on by stress.

31

I held the grocery bag close to my chest as protection against the bitter wind that had picked up since I'd left work over an hour ago. In addition to cat food, I bought a few frozen dinners. I'd have one on Thanksgiving; a Thanksgiving I'd spend alone.

The wind whipped my hair across my face. I hadn't cut it in two years. Maybe it was time for a trim, but Dane always loved it long. Cutting it made me somehow feel that I would be cutting Dane from my memory. Ends that he touched, chopped off and swept away forever.

I reached my townhouse and, still clutching the bag, managed to unlock the door. The phone was ringing as I entered. Groaning, I set the bag down and rushed to answer it. It was probably my mother, trying for the hundredth time to change my mind about not joining the family for Thanksgiving dinner.

Yep, the ID system showed my parents' number. If I didn't answer, she'd keep calling, and then she'd worry. I lifted the receiver and punched the talk button. "Hello Mom."

"Nina, your father and I are still very upset about you not coming for Thanksgiving."

Just like Mom, I thought, getting right to the point. "Mom, I can't face everyone. I told you that. I'll stay home, relax, and make myself something to eat. Ebony will be with me, so I won't be alone."

She snorted. "Thanksgiving with a cat. Really, Nina, Thanksgiving is for family. It'll be different than last year. You're not going to be treated with kid gloves again. You need it this year. You need it to heal, to be with your family. Grandmom is cooking ravioli and meatballs just the way you like them, and you know how much you love my turkey and stuffing. Glenn and Lanie will be here. Deidra is bringing her new boyfriend and a coworker of hers who just moved to the area. Everyone will be here. You can't stay home alone and wallow in pity. We won't let you."

Sadness washed over me and I squeezed the telephone. "Mom, maybe I am wallowing, but I can't handle being around Glenn and Lanie, seeing them kissing and cooing, talking incessantly about the baby's arrival next month." My chest tightened. "And Deidra with a new boyfriend. She's always in love with someone. It's all too much happiness for me right now. You'll be better off if I don't come."

"Don't be ridiculous," Mom said. "Glenn's your brother. He loves you. We all do."

"Mom, I can't."

"Nina, you're a beautiful, intelligent young woman. You're only thirty, for God's sake. Dane would want you to live."

"Mom, I can't talk about Dane."

"Dear," she said, her voice softer. "You need to talk about him.

It's not healthy keeping your grief bottled up. I'm here for you."

"I know, Mom, and I don't want to hurt you or Dad, but I have to do what I think is right for me now."

A scratching noise by the door snagged my attention and I looked over. I'd left the front door slightly ajar in my haste to answer the phone. Ebony was poking at the door with her paw. She opened it just enough to slip through.

"No, Ebony, come back!" I shouted. An indoor cat, lately she'd found ways to escape, sometimes disappearing for a full day.

"Mom, gotta go. Call you later." I threw down the phone and grabbed my keys. I locked up quickly and ran out. The heck with the frozen foods in the shopping bag; Ebony was more important.

I lifted my coat collar against the brisk wind and hurried down the street, my glance searching under bushes as I walked. Leaves swirled by me, and in the distance a dog's bark carried clearly in the crisp air, as if heralding harsher weather to come.

"Ebony!" I called. Dusk was mantling the tightly packed townhouse community. A black cat could blend in easily. Fear made my throat thicken. Ebony wasn't street smart. She was timid, afraid of everything. A week ago some workmen had left my door open and Ebony had gotten out. Since then, she'd found ways to escape every chance she got. I wondered what so enticed her to keep running away.

A few houses down, I saw a door open. I'd heard someone new had moved in the house that had been vacant a while, but I'd not seen him or her yet. A man, tall and wide-shouldered, stood silhouetted by the light that spilled out. He looked down. I followed his gaze and saw my cat, her tail held high, sauntering through his door. He quickly closed it.

Anger hit me. That man had my Ebony. I straightened my shoulders and marched up to the house. I rapped on the door, hard.

The door opened immediately. My breath hitched. Aquamarine eyes met mine. A lock of dark curly hair fell over a high, very masculine forehead. The handsome stranger from the supermarket looked shocked, then his lips curved into a smile.

Awareness flashed in his eyes for an instant. "We meet again." He quirked one beautiful black eyebrow. "Are you following me?" His voice teased. "I like it, having a beautiful woman follow me."

I bristled. "Of course I'm not following you. I live a few houses down. You have my cat."

He frowned. "Blackie is your cat?"

"Blackie? You call a black cat Blackie?"

He laughed, a smoky sound that sent excitement swirling through me. "Not very creative of me, is it?" He stepped back. "Please come in."

I hesitated a second. I didn't know this man. But a part of me wanted to know him. And he had my cat. I threw aside my apprehensions and entered.

I spotted Ebony on the black leather sofa, calmly washing herself. "Ebony, what are you doing here?"

She looked up at me with large yellow eyes, as if to say, I belong here. Why are you here?

I walked over and picked her up, holding her close. "She's an indoor cat," I said, turning to my handsome neighbor. He watched me, a gleam of admiration in his eyes. Heat spread from my neck to my face, and I held Ebony closer. "She's been escaping the house lately and I've been wondering where she goes.

"She showed up on my doorstep last week, the day I moved in. I thought she'd been abandoned." He walked toward me. "I'm sorry. If I'd known she belonged to you, I would have taken her back. Since then, she comes and goes." He smiled a little sheepishly. "I even went out and bought her some food."

He held out a hand. "I'm Jeremy Donovan, by the way."

Still holding Ebony, I took his hand. When our hands touched, an electrical charge, sensual and scorching, traveled up my arm. From the glint in his eyes, I knew he felt it too. No man had ever incited this sort of instant attraction in me, not even Dane.

Frightened and excited at the same time, I shook Jeremy's hand and quickly released it. "Nina Mercier," I said. Straightening, I willed myself to get a grip. I didn't even know this man, yet his nearness somehow made my heart, dead as the leaves outside, seem to spring to life again.

He smiled a slow, sexy smile that curled my toes. "Nina, in honor of our neighborly meeting and our mutual admiration for Blackie, uh, Ebony, please stay and chat. Would you like a drink?"

Since Dane died, I'd shielded my heart from everyone. Friends had tried to set me up on dates, but I refused out of loyalty to Dane. But this wasn't a date, I told myself. This is simply two neighbors having a friendly drink.

Jeremy watched me with an expectant look on his ruggedly handsome face. Something inside me loosened, releasing a little bit of the pain that had held me hostage for the past two years.

"A drink sounds good. Thanks."

"Great. Have a seat. I can take your coat," he said, gesturing one hand to the couch, then to me.

I placed Ebony back on the leather sofa and slipped off my heavy coat, handing it to Jeremy. Too nervous to sit, I walked around the room. Although furnished in a very masculine style with a black leather sofa and chair set, the room exuded warmth and comfort.

34

Books crowded shelves set beside the fireplace. Magazines were strewn over the glass-topped coffee table. I stole a glance at the covers—news and financial magazines stacked next to law journals. A lawyer?

"I hope white wine is okay," he said, entering the room with two crystal wine goblets and an unopened bottle. I was relieved. I still didn't know him very well and had a thing about accepting opened beverages from men.

"White's fine." I watched as he unscrewed the cork and poured the gold fluid into our glasses. I took the glass from him. Our fingers touched, and another bolt of electricity shot through me. In all the years I'd known Dane, I'd never once felt this sensual appeal that sent hot-cold shivers over me. I sipped my wine, hoping the rich liquid would calm me.

"Tell me about yourself, Nina Mercier." He looked down at my left hand, which was wrapped around the wine goblet. "What do you do?"

"I teach fifth grade."

"A teacher. Great profession," he said with a nod. "Please sit. I think Blackie, I mean Ebony, wants to stay a while."

I looked over to where my cat slept peacefully curled up on the sofa. Traitor, I wanted to shout. She seemed perfectly at home here.

I sipped wine and sank down onto the soft leather next to my cat. Jeremy sat across from me in one of the comfortable looking recliners.

"Are you married?" he asked. "Engaged?"

I widened my eyes. "You're not too subtle, are you?"

He laughed. "No. I've learned there's too much time wasted in being subtle. When I left you in the parking lot, I wanted to kick myself for not getting your phone number." He lifted his glass in salute. "And here we are. Do you believe in fate, Nina?"

Fate. Shivers ran over me. Was it fate that Dane would die the day before our wedding?

I looked at Jeremy. "No, I don't believe in fate."

His gaze softened and he studied me as if he could see inside to my core. "What is it, Nina? Do you wanna talk about whatever put that sadness into your beautiful brown eyes?"

This is a new pickup line, I thought. Yet, there was a sensitivity to Jeremy's eyes that told me he'd glimpsed the sorrow that resided in me. Maybe it was the wine, maybe it was the gentle way Jeremy studied me, or maybe it was the fact that tomorrow was the anniversary of Dane's death. Something in Jeremy reached out to me. I'd held my grief for two years now. I'd never discussed my feelings with my mother or my friends. Whatever the reason, I felt compelled to unburden my soul to this man.

35

I released a shaky breath. "I was to be married last Thanksgiving, but my fiancé was killed in a car accident the day before." I gripped my wine glass, as if it could give me courage.

Jeremy watched me for what felt like minutes, his expression soft.

What had gotten into me? I didn't want or need anyone's pity. I put my half-finished glass of wine on the coffee table and stood. "I'd better go."

He stood too and reached out to touch my hand. "Don't. I suspect you need to talk. Please stay. Tell me about your fiancé."

I hesitated. I wanted to talk, needed to talk at last. My gaze on his, I sat down again and clasped my hands on my lap. "Dane and I were high school sweethearts. We always knew we would marry. College and careers interfered, and then we were finally able to have our wedding." I reached over and began petting Ebony, not looking at Jeremy. Ebony purred, the sound calming me. "But we never had that chance."

Jeremy left his chair and came to sit next to me, taking my hand in his. "I'm sorry, Nina."

Either he was very good at seduction, or he was truly sorry. I looked into his eyes and saw sympathy and understanding—an awareness that spoke to an answering awareness I felt deep in my center.

He stroked my hand. Heat wrapped around my heart. I could learn to like this man. No, I couldn't be disloyal to Dane. I pulled free.

"You're a beautiful woman, Nina," he said, his voice husky. "I didn't know your fiancé, but I'm sure he loved you enough to want you to move on."

I shook my head. "I've said more than I should have." I lifted my chin. "I've told you about me. Now it's your turn. Are you married? Engaged?"

Pain flashed over his features for a second. He tensed and leaned back in his seat. "Divorced. She left me for my best friend."

I twisted around to look at him. "Jeremy, I'm so sorry."

He waved a hand. "Don't be. That was three years ago. I'm over it."

I remembered the pain that slashed his features. I wasn't so sure he was over it. "Tell me about it," I said softly. I settled into my seat, somehow comfortable with this man I barely knew. Dane and I used to share our thoughts and feelings. But unlike with Dane, undercurrents of sensuality vibrated between Jeremy and I. I didn't understand it and wouldn't try to, at least not now.

It was several minutes before he spoke. Then when he did, his voice was so low I had to strain to hear. He stared straight ahead.

36

"At first, when I learned of their betrayal, I didn't care about anything, even living. Before the divorce was finalized, I quit my job and cut ties with everyone I knew. Then I traveled the world, doing the most dangerous things I could think of. Jumping out of airplanes, mountain climbing, rock climbing. I think I had a death wish."

I reached out and touched his hand. "Oh, Jeremy."

He turned to me with a slight smile. "Kind of foolish, huh? But I got everything out of my system, decided I really didn't want to die, and that maybe there was another woman out there for me, someone who I could truly love—someone who would love me. So I went home."

"Home is here in Delaware?"

"Minnesota."

"How did you end up here?"

He shrugged. "A job offer I couldn't refuse. A chance to start over."

"What happened to your ex-wife?"

He chuckled. "What goes around, comes around, as they say. Her lover cheated on her. She called me right before I moved out here, wanting to reconcile."

"Do you still love her?" For some reason that I couldn't explain, I had to know the answer.

His blue-green eyes bore into mine. "No."

A small kernel of hope opened in me. I quickly suppressed it. My thoughts made me disloyal to Dane.

Jeremy reached out and skimmed a finger over my bottom lip. "My grief wasn't as bad as yours, but I learned to get over it and live again. You need to do that too, Nina."

I quickly stood. "I think I'd better leave."

Jeremy stood also. Only a whisper separated us. I inhaled his scent of citrus and the outdoors.

He bent his head toward me. "You are very beautiful, Nina Mercier."

I knew he was going to kiss me. And God help me, I wanted him to. I lifted my face toward his.

His lips touched mine, tentative at first, then growing more confident, more demanding. His kiss cajoled and seduced. Waves of need washed over me. I pressed closer and wrapped my arms around his neck. Groaning softly, I opened my mouth to his sensual probing. Warmth seeped into my belly and lower.

A door slammed somewhere outside, dragging me back to reality. What would Dane say? I wasn't being true to him. I jerked away.

Jeremy and I looked at each other, our breathing ragged. He raked fingers through his thick hair. "I can't say I'm sorry, Nina. I've wanted to kiss you since I saw you in the supermarket parking lot."

"I need to go." I grabbed my coat and a startled Ebony and marched to the door.

I turned the doorknob, but Jeremy touched my arm, stopping me. He gently pulled me around to face him.

"I want to see you again," he said.

I shook my head. "That's not possible."

I looked at Jeremy and envisioned a future, a future open to love again, to possibilities. No, I couldn't betray Dane. I opened the door and slid out. Holding Ebony close, I strode quickly away. I felt Jeremy watching. I'd allowed him to kiss me, had wanted him to kiss me. I'd been unfaithful to Dane's memory. How could I have lost control like that?

But I knew.

From the first moment I'd looked into Jeremy's eyes, something deep and yearning had pulsed through me. No one had ever before incited such an instant response in me. Dane had been my friend, comfortable and familiar. If we had no great passion, so be it. We knew each other well, complemented each other. I didn't need passion.

But Jeremy was different. He made me want him with an aching need that threatened my control. He wouldn't be easily handled or easily dismissed. He was danger. Excitement skittered over me.

I wanted to see Jeremy again, wanted to taste him, feel him. My controlled world began to spin away.

For the first time in two years, I felt tears building. I ran the rest of the way home.

I quickly unlocked the door and slid in, shutting the door and leaning against it. I dropped my coat on the floor and hugged a squirming Ebony to me, inhaling her sweet scent and rubbing my face in her silky fur.

"What have I done, Ebony?"

The tears burst forth, a torrent of grief dammed up for too long. My shoulders shook with my sobs. I buried my head in Ebony's fur and poured out my despair, my anger, my unhappiness until there were no more tears to give.

Finally I released the cat and wiped fingers over my damp face. I felt lighter, more hopeful than I had in a long time. A part of me would always love Dane, but maybe it was time to move on.

You look good, Nina, if I do say so myself." I twirled in the mirror, looking at my image from every angle. I wanted to look my best today when I joined my family for Thanksgiving. I studied my sleek brown pants and riding boots. The deep purple of my cashmere sweater complimented my black hair and brown eyes. I flipped back strands of hair. Dane had always loved my hair. Tears threatened to spring forth, and I blinked them back. Dane would have wanted me to go on, to have a life, to have the children I'd always wanted.

I wondered what Jeremy was doing today. He'd been in my thoughts all day yesterday as I taught my excited class of fifth graders. With turkey and stuffing and all the trimmings on their minds, my students had been a handful. I was glad when school ended. I loved them, but I looked forward to a long holiday away from them.

Will I see Jeremy over the weekend? I narrowed my eyes at myself in the mirror. Maybe I should be bold and march up to his house and ask him out. My face reddened. No, I wasn't ready for that yet. But I'd dreamt about Jeremy, an erotic dream that woke me in a sweat, on fire for him. My body tightened, remembering his sexual magnetism and his kiss the other night. I rubbed a finger over my lips, recalling the feel of his firm lips moving softly, yet forcefully, over mine.

Shoving aside the dangerous thoughts of Jeremy, I grabbed my large brown purse from the chair and strode from the bedroom, pretending a confidence I didn't feel. I could do this, I told myself. Time for a new beginning. There had to be another man out there for me. A small voice whispered, But no one as attractive and sexy as Jeremy. I ignored the voice.

Mom had almost cried when I called her yesterday to tell her I'd be at Thanksgiving dinner after all. I would get through the day knowing I'd made my mother happy.

Ebony sat washing herself at the sunshine-filled bay window. "I've got to go," I told her, stroking her soft fur. "I'll bring you some turkey."

She blinked her yellow eyes. I could swear she understood me.

My parents gave me huge hugs and kisses when I arrived. Grandmom, her hands white with flour, kissed me on both cheeks. Basking in the warmth of family, I began to relax. The scents of turkey and stuffing and sweet potatoes further calmed me, bringing me back to happy times when Dane joined our family for Thanksgiving. I took a glass of wine from my dad and shook off my melancholy. Today was a new beginning.

Glenn and Lanie were the first to arrive. They burst into the living room, bringing love riding on a blast of cold air.

Glenn doted on his pregnant wife. The love shining between them filled me with bittersweet yearning. But I would not allow my grief to ruin this day for anyone.

Glenn hugged me. His eyes searched mine. "How are you, Nina?"

I hugged him back. "I'm fine, Glenn, I really am."

Lanie hugged me next, her hard belly pressing against me. "You look amazing."

39

"Thanks, but you're the one who's amazing." I held her at arm's length. "Pregnancy becomes you."

She laughed and pressed a hand to her belly. "I feel so fat."

"You're beautiful," Glenn said, coming up behind his wife and planting a kiss on the back of her neck.

Aching loneliness rushed through me and I stepped away.

The doorbell rang.

"That must be Deidra with her new boyfriend and friend," Mom said, hurrying to open the door.

Deidra, brown eyes sparkling and long black hair brushing her shoulders, walked in, followed by two men.

Shock sucked the air from me as my gaze collided with aquamarine eyes. Jeremy stared at me, his eyes wide.

Anger pierced me. Which one was Deidra's new boyfriend? Was it Jeremy? Really, what a fool I'd been. Just my luck, mooning over a two-timer. I barely looked at the other man with them.

"Aunt Rose, Uncle Ted," Deidra gushed, hugging my parents. She turned to me and took my hands, holding them between hers, still cold from the outdoors. "Nina, you look great. I'm so glad to see you." Her eyes turned soft. "How are you holding up?"

I bristled. I knew she meant well, but she was with Jeremy. "I'm doing okay."

She planted a light kiss on my cheek, then hugged Glenn and Lanie.

Grandmom came out of the kitchen, and Deidra ran to her and grabbed her in a bear hug that made Grandmom laugh.

Beaming, and holding onto Grandmom's arm, Deidra's gaze swept us. "I'd like you all to meet a man who is very special to me."

Jealousy and hurt knotted my stomach. I squared my shoulders. Jeremy had played me. I would not allow him to know the humiliation I felt.

Releasing Grandmom, Deidra approached Jeremy and the other man. I noticed the other guy for the first time. Slim and blond, with even, handsome features, his worshipful gaze locked on Deidra. I felt so embarrassed that I was sure my cheeks were bright pink. I'd been so negative and cynical since Dane's death. I thought for sure that I was destined for loneliness—that true love only came around once, and once it's gone, it's gone. Since I already used up my voucher, I didn't think I'd get another chance, but really, I'd been too afraid to stand in line and buy one—resigning myself to a love-free, celibate life. It was all becoming too clear.

Deidra went to the blond man and took his arm, drawing him to her side. "Grandmom, Aunt Rose, Uncle Ted, everyone, this is Neil. He and I—." Her face pinked. "Well, he means a lot to me."

I felt someone watching and turned to see Jeremy staring at me, his gaze hot. An answering fire sparked low in my gut, and I quickly looked away.

Deidra finished her introductions to Neil, then gestured to Jeremy. "This is Jeremy Donovan. He just joined our firm. He's from Minnesota, he's a great lawyer, and he doesn't know anyone here. I didn't want him to spend Thanksgiving alone."

"Welcome, Jeremy," Mom said. "We're glad Deidra invited you. We wouldn't want you to spend Thanksgiving alone either."

Jeremy shook hands all around. When he reached me, he held my hand a trifle longer than was necessary. As before, a sensual charge passed between us.

"Good to see you again, Nina," he said, his voice low and seductive. "Do you believe in fate now?"

I swallowed the dryness in my throat. "I think I might."

"You two know each other?" Mom asked.

Jeremy turned to Mom. "We're neighbors. We met the other night." He looked down at me. "A very smart cat introduced us."

My face burned and I looked at Mom. Her eyes glinted. I knew that look—matchmaker mode.

I snatched my hand from Jeremy's. I didn't need my mother interfering with my love life—the love life I was going to try for.

After dinner, we women sat in the den and talked while the men cleared dishes and cleaned the kitchen. I loved this part of our Thanksgiving tradition. Married on Thanksgiving thirty-five years ago, my dad promised my mom he would never abandon her to watch football on Thanksgiving. He'd kept his word, going further by insisting she relax while he cleaned up.

I looked at my mom, her face unlined, her eyes sparkling with happiness. She and my dad had a storybook marriage. Once I'd dreamed of a loving, fairytale marriage with Dane.

I'd always known Dane and I would have a comfortable life together. But meeting Jeremy made me realize I didn't want comfort. I wanted passion—hot, sizzling, mind-blowing passion. The thought made my cheeks burn, and I quickly tossed back the last of my wine and set the empty glass on the coffee table with a loud thump.

"Nina, are you okay?" Mom asked.

I frowned. "I'm fine. Why?"

"You've been different today, kind of edgy and distracted."

Deidra laughed. "She's hot for Jeremy. She's got it bad. Anyone could see that."

I flared my nostrils. "I'm not hot for anyone."

"Yes, you are," Deidra said. "It's nothing to be ashamed of. You deserve some happiness. Go for it, Nina."

"I think Jeremy is hot for Nina," Lanie said. "Did you notice the way he looked at her through dinner?" She sat in the rocking chair, smiling like the Cheshire cat and rubbing her swollen belly.

"Stop it, all of you," I said.

"Jeremy seems like a very nice young man," Mom said.

"I think so too," Grandmom echoed.

Dad came into the den, saving me from further embarrassment. "Cleanup's done." He looked at Mom with love in his eyes. "You know what that means."

Smiling, she got up and went to stand beside him. Glenn came into the den and popped a CD into the player.

Then Jeremy and Neil crowded into the room. Jeremy's gaze found mine. We stared at each other. The air in the room grew thick.

"What's going on?" Neil asked.

"Mom and Dad were married on Thanksgiving," Glenn answered. "So each Thanksgiving, they play the song they danced to at their wedding, and they dance again."

The lilting tune promising sultry nights and everlasting love began to play. Dad took Mom in his arms and they danced around the den. We stood and watched. Tears filled my eyes. My parents had a beautiful marriage, and a deeply passionate one, evident by the way they held each other. I wanted it all, the love and the passion.

I looked over to see Jeremy watching me again. Something hot passed between us. I walked slowly toward him.

He put his hand on my shoulder when I reached him. His touch seared me beneath the cashmere. "Let's take a walk," he whispered.

Our coats on, scarves wrapped around our necks, we held hands and walked into the cold night. Our breath mingled in the clear air. Lights shone in the houses we passed, and I imagined happy families sharing their Thanksgiving meals.

A light snow began to fall. Laughing, I looked up at Jeremy. "Look, it's snowing. It's beautiful."

He pulled me close. His gaze searched mine, then he reached out and skimmed a finger over my lips. I shivered in delicious anticipation.

"You're beautiful," he whispered. "I like your parents' tradition of the Thanksgiving dance."

"I do too," I said.

"Nina, are you willing to take a chance on me, on us?" Light from the streetlamp reflected on his incredible eyes, eyes that looked at me with longing and hope. Snowflakes glistened on his black hair. "I promise to do all I can to make you happy."

I blinked back tears and nodded.

"Let's start our own Thanksgiving tradition," he said, his voice husky.

He took me in his arms, holding me close, and waltzed me around the street. His leather jacket was soft against my cheek, and his heart beat sure and steady. We danced with the snow falling gently—the quiet surrounding us. We had no music, but I heard music in my heart—healing music, loving music, hopeful music.

Jeremy stopped and looked down at me. He bent his head and took my lips in a soft kiss. My heart sang. I'd found my way home again, home for Thanksgiving—to a future filled with promise.

THE END

A LESSON LEARNED
A Poor Man's Sacrifice Taught Me
The Real Meaning Of Thanksgiving

Thanksgiving! And food shopping was horrendous. I'd debated with myself all day if I should stop at the local fast-food restaurant for my usual order of curry chicken, or if I should do some minimal shopping at the supermarket. Typically, I had intended to get only two or three things, thus making me a prime candidate for the eight-or-less item checkout line. But before I knew it, on-sale items that I really didn't need, seemed to magically jump into my cart.

My heart sank as I headed toward the checkout line and saw the people leisurely standing in place—one behind the other—wending in abstract lines, thumbing through magazines as they waited to be rung up. I knew it would be a while, so, like everyone else, I reached for the one of those mendacious little tabloids.

I didn't notice the man directly in front of me until it was time for him to be rung up. It wasn't so much him, but the way the cashier was talking to him.

"Fourteen-sixty-four," she'd said, looking at him with impatience.

He stopped bagging his groceries and opened his wallet, drawing out two bills: a ten and two singles. The cashier's mouth was a severe, and clearly exasperated line. I saw him looking at the few, mostly generic, seemingly necessary items.

"I'll have to put something back," he mumbled.

The irritable groans of the shoppers behind me, and the way the cashier pounded on the bell at the side of the register signaling for a manager, made my blood boil.

Before I knew it, I reached into my purse and drew out a five-dollar bill.

"Here!" I exclaimed, almost shoving it at her.

The cashier took the bill with a smirk, made change, letting her hand dangle in mid-air between the man and me. He looked at the change for what seemed like many seconds, then without a single word, he just snatched his bag and hurried out of the store while the cashier rang up my items with a derisive grin. Ordinarily, I'd have bagged my groceries, but I was determined to make her work after witnessing her nasty disposition.

I grabbed up my bag and walked out the door.

Outside, I saw the man in a dingy white station wagon. Two

44

small children sat next to him, forcing slices of white bread into their mouths. He looked up and saw me, his own mouth filled, halting in mid-chew. He cranked up the car, which coughed and spewed black smoke from the tailpipe, before it finally kicked into gear and sped away.

On a crisp cold evening, after getting off the bus near my apartment, I walked home gazing at the brightly adorned stores and houses. I must have walked past Holy Sacrament church a thousand times over the years, but that night, as the chilly air whipped around the hem of my warm coat, I heard the muffled sound of singing. The closer I got, the louder it became. It was children's voices singing one of my favorite hymns. I found myself climbing the wide stone steps of the old church, the sound of those voices drawing me in.

Inside, it was peaceful as I loosened my scarf, and walked toward the pews. I glanced at the pitifully few people that dotted the seats. Couples, singles, and people who'd just come in to get out of the cold. Down near the altar, a tall, thin man was conducting youngsters in song while the organist accompanied. The young voices lowered to a hum, and suddenly, the church was filled with a strong soprano voice singing the melody. I looked at the face of the young girl who appeared to be about twelve. She was thin—far too thin for such a powerful voice to emanate from such a frail-looking frame. I was mesmerized by the beautiful voice of this young girl. At the end of the song, there was a smattering of applause as the children picked up the beat with a livelier song.

Following a brief prayer, the offering plate was passed. I was appalled and ashamed by the meager contributions that lay in the plate. I pulled out the four tens and eight singles and dropped them in. A myriad of feelings washed over me: sadness, joy and peace. For the first time since I was a girl, I prayed.

I don't know how long I stayed there with my head bowed when I heard a voice.

"Did you see me, Daddy?"

It was the young singer, and she had run into her father's open arms.

"I sure did, honey; you were wonderful," he said.

I gasped when I saw him; it was the man from the store!

He put the girl down, and began to button her coat. He pulled the scarf snugly around her head and neck.

"Where's James?"

"He didn't feel too good, honey. He's at home; we best hurry."

Unable to help myself, like a thief, I stole behind them as they walked out into the cold night. I was sure his battered pile of junk was parked nearby, but he just tucked his daughter's hand into his pocket—along with his own gloveless palm. Together, they speed-

45

walked down the dark street. I followed them for seven blocks in the bone-chilling cold until finally, he reached a dilapidated building with broken panes in the front door. As they disappeared inside, I walked up the cracked concrete steps and peered into the dingy glass. I watched his back as he opened a door at the far end of the hall and let his daughter in, first. Slowly, he began to turn around. I ducked away just in the nick of time—positive he hadn't seen me.

I didn't sleep much that night. My mind was running a gamut of thoughts ranging from disgust to pity.

I awakened to a bleak and uncharacteristically cold Thanksgiving morning. I turned on the gourmet coffee pot I'd purchased only months before—along with every flavor of coffee they sold—but I was edgy. Something was bothering me. Almost like an itch I couldn't scratch, I needed to do something, but I had no idea what. I tried to read the newspaper, but I couldn't concentrate.

Then, an article caught my eye: Please help, only $2.49 will provide one meal for a homeless person on Thanksgiving Day.

I got up, dialed information, and asked for the nearest soup kitchen. After the operator gave me the number, I dialed it, and a harried voice answered.

"First Street Sanctuary! Can I help you?"

"Hi, my name is Candace Dawkins, and I was wondering—"

Before I could finish, the woman was firing off the address of the place. She told me that the holiday meal would be served all day, or until the food ran out. She was about to end the conversation with a routinely practiced "have a nice- day," when I broke in.

"I was wondering if you needed any help, today?"

There was a long silence on the other end.

"What did you say?"

Her voice was incredulous.

"Do you need any help down at the food kitchen, today?"

She told me that the 49th Street Kitchen across town was badly in need of volunteers. She took my name, and told me she'd call them so that they'd be expecting me. After she gave me the address, I dressed in a long woolen skirt and a warm, high-necked sweater, and off I went to catch the crosstown bus. I wanted to feel good about what I was about to do, but I didn't, because that was something I should have been doing all along.

As I got off the bus and walked toward the soup shelter, I could already see a line of people bunched together—shifting from foot to foot in order to keep warm. I hurried to the back entrance, and rang the bell. After a few moments, the door opened a crack, and a barely perceptible face peeked through.

"Hi I'm Candace Dawkins."

46

The grizzled man looked at me, then at a dog-eared yellow ruled pad that hung on the door frame. He widened the door, and I stepped in. As peaceful as the church had been the day before, this was the exact opposite. People were hurrying from place to place, carrying large quantities of all different types of food, trays, and drinks.

"Hi! I'm Jobo—short for Joseph Bonner. Thanks for coming down."

I was surprised to see a man in his early twenties with white, even teeth, and a shock of dark, thick wavy hair smiling at me. He was ushering me along, helping me off with my coat, and chattering on about what needed to be done. It was as though he had three sets of hands, because not a moment or gesture was wasted. Each time he passed a station, he touched, straightened, or poured as he continued to brief me.

"Okay! why don't you start outside with the tables. We ask everyone to empty their own trays, but sometimes, they forget."

He handed me a spray bottle, a pair of lightweight rubber gloves, and a cloth. He tied an apron around me, and pointed toward the swinging door.

"Oh! And Candace. . . ." I turned to look at him. "Thanks for coming down."

I felt the heat of a blush creep up my face, something else I hadn't done for years.

Outside, the tables were filled with people. Whole families of people. Mothers with children, mothers and fathers with their children. Singles, homeless people, even aging prostitutes who sat alongside strangers eating what probably amounted as the only meal of their entire day.

I cleaned the tables and emptied trays. I helped the seniors and handicapped get seated, and brought food to those who were unable to do it for themselves. The line seemed endless with black faces, white faces, faces etched with pain, despair—and in some cases, a little madness. But they were all there for the same reason: They were hungry.

"Candace!" JoBo exclaimed, "We need you take over at the serving station."

I hurried to the kitchen.

"You'll be serving at this station. It's one scoop of potatoes, a dollop of cranberry sauce, a slice of bread, and a ladle of gravy. I don't care how hungry they look, that's it," Jobo instructed as he placed some thin turkey slices onto a plastic plate.

My face must have shown some baffled concern because his voice lowered and softened.

"I'm not being harsh, Candace, we have a lot of people to feed, and we have to make the food last as long as possible. And while you're at it, give 'em a smile. Too many people treat them like they're

47

invisible, but don't patronize them with well-meaning conversation. Okay?"

"I understand Jobo."

For the next hour, I served the food. There were so many desperate, sad faces. I wondered if people out in the world knew just how lucky they were to be surrounded by a loving family, eating a nice Thanksgiving meal in a cozy warm house or apartment.

"I like cranberry sauce."

A familiar little voice brought me back from my dreamy thoughts. I was shocked as I looked down into the half-smiling face of the little girl that had sung in church the night before.

"It's one of my favorites, too."

I grinned back at her and put an extra dollop on her plate. I could feel the chastising eyes of the server next to me, and I didn't dare look up. I served the little boy, next—whom I assumed was her brother. My eyes continued traveling to the man beside them. It was he all right—the man from the grocery store. His face was tired, and he kept his eyes trained on the tray.

"Happy Thanksgiving," I said, softly.

His eyes dragged up from the tray of food and stared into mine. His cold, hard look said it all, and I hated myself for having said the most absolutely stupid thing in the world.

As I thought further, I couldn't remember hearing anyone utter that sentiment the entire time I had been there.

This was not Thanksgiving. To them, it was just another day—a day when they got a special dish of food. Food that was donated by people who had more than they could use.

The little group moved on and sat at an empty table. The man began to dip into the plate hungrily, but the young girl said something to him, and then folded her thin little hands in prayer. I apologized to the server next to me about the cranberry sauce.

"Don't worry, honey, ain't a one of us who ain't done the same thing the first time out."

I had no idea how I was going to get through the rest of the day with sights like those, but I knew if they could stand their lives the way they were, then I could certainly tolerate a little patience and understanding.

It was nine o'clock, and the flow of people had ebbed with just a few remaining itinerants scraping the last bits of food from the plastic dishes into their mouths.

Jobo and the others had already set the kitchen to rights, and were preparing things for the next day's crew.

"Night everybody!" Jobo said, waving as he left through the front door of the food shelter.

I felt a little funny. What was I expecting? Gratitude? I shook off the negative feeling that was creeping up my spine, and I went to get my coat and headed out the door. It wasn't the safest part of town, and I thought I'd better look for a cab instead of waiting for the bus.

"Excuse me."

Startled, I turned. It was the man from inside.

"I was . . . well, what I mean to say is we . . . were wondering if you needed a ride—it being so late and all," he said in a low voice.

The cynical part of me was screaming out a warning, but my sympathetic self was telling me that I had insulted this man enough.

"I'd love a ride."

He led the way to the car where his two kids were in the back seat. James was fast asleep. His sister was wide-awake, but bundled close to him. The man opened the car door for me, and I slid into the front seat. After he'd closed it, I turned to the young girl.

"Hi, I'm Candace."

"I'm Janelle," she said, wisps of vaporous breath escaping from her mouth.

Her father got in quickly, slamming the door shutting out the cold air. He cranked up the car. It sputtered and faltered.

"Come on, please. . . ." I heard him whisper as he pumped the gas pedal. Finally, the car sprang to life.

"Here we go." He pulled away from the curb. "Where do you live?"

"Over on Twenty-sixth Street, but you don't have to go all the way over there, I don't want to take you out of your way."

"Nonsense, it's cold out, and it's on the way. But I'm sure you already know that."

My face flushed with embarrassment. So! He had seen me when I looked into the broken dirty glass of his apartment building the night before. He pulled up in front of my building, and stopped the car.

"Thanks for the ride; there's no telling when I would have gotten a cab." I winced again. Another luxury taken for granted. "By the way, I'm Candace Dawkins"

"Marc Hudson, you've met Janelle. The sleeping one is James."

"Well, thanks again for the ride."

"Look, about that day in the store, I . . . I . . . really meant to thank you, and I intend to pay you back . . . but . . . "

He choked up and couldn't go on.

I wanted to say it was okay, and that the real reason I'd done it, had been for my own gratification against the rude cashier. This man had pride; I could see that.

"You've more than paid it back with this ride."

I opened the door to let myself out. Just as I was about to close it,

"Candace! Happy Thanksgiving," Marc said and smiled.

Every part of me was tingling as I entered my building. Inside my apartment, I looked at my answering machine, and there were three messages. My hand flew to my mouth because I knew all of them had to be from my mother whom I had forgotten to call. I played them back. Sure enough, the first one was the obligatory where are you? The second was "I'm a little worried, where are you?" The last was the "Fine! Leave your mother all alone on Thanksgiving Day" guilt call.

It was late, but I dialed her number, anyway.

"Mother. . . ." I said when she picked up after the first ring.

"I've met the most unusual man."

I ran into Marc on several occasions doing odd Jobs in and around the neighborhood. He smiled, but never stopped to talk.

Christmas had come and gone, and New Year's Eve was approaching. I saw Marc delivering pizzas to a nearby apartment building, and I asked him if he and the kids would like to come over for dinner, and to watch the ball at Times Square drop, heralding a brand new year.

"They'd like that; me too!"

The kids never made it to midnight. They were long asleep on my bed where they had been watching the Wizard Of Oz.

Marc and I talked right up until the ball fell. He told me about his wife who'd passed away two years before, and it had devastated him. After her death, his company downsized him out of the job he'd held for more than fifteen years.

"I worked all my life. I went to college at night and earned my degree, so I could continue to provide for my family," he said, choking up.

But he explained that none of it mattered when you had two mouths to feed, and the conglomerates with their takeovers and nepotistic practices wanted you out. They didn't care that families were left with no medical benefits, their accustomed lifestyle changed, nor the fact that the severance would run out, and how hard it would be to find a job for which he was suited.

"Companies don't want long-term employees, anymore. Corporate America just wasn't interested in the loyalty and longevity I'd given. The new world is five terms at the most, and then out you go," he said, bitterly.

I could see how much it sickened Marc to talk about it, and it nearly broke my heart.

"I'm not a loser, Candace. Just because there was no more work, didn't mean I had no worth. I did every job they threw at me. I took myself to computer classes, and I learned. Then, they tossed me out— and at a time when I was least able to cope!"

50

I wanted to tell him that it was just business, and all of the companies were doing it. But that was too easy when I was graced with a great job and excellent benefits.

"I'm sorry you had to go through all that, Marc."

"I never gave a second thought to how women have to take care of the kids, work, and run a household. How'd they do it? Kids bickering, having to go school to sort out some problem or another with their teacher. Accidents, hospitalization, colds—the works."

I laughed a little.

"You're just getting a taste of what women have had to go through since the beginning of time."

I was suddenly looking into deep, dark eyes. He was handsome in a strong, earthy way. His face showed wear, but how could it not with all he'd endured and all that he was facing?

"I think it's time to get the kids and head home," he said, after realizing my scrutiny.

"Why not let them sleep here? You can stay, too."

"Perhaps another time," he said softly, his eyes staring straight into mine.

He went into my room and gently shook Janelle awake. There was no way James was going to budge, so he gathered the little boy up in arms, who whimpered sleepily, and wound his arms about his father's neck.

"Thank you; this was a treat for the kids—and for me," he whispered at the door.

I began to get close to Janelle and James, and they were growing fond of me, too. Marc was looking for permanent work, but was only able to find odd jobs that were nowhere near his potential.

A few days later, I had a business lunch with some clients at a popular eatery near the office. "May I take your order please?" The familiar voice resounded in my ears as I looked up at Marc. His face remained stoic as he answered the client's request for the specials of the day. Marc rattled them off as I was to speak to him, but his eyes told me no!

Shortly after that episode, I went out-of-town on business, and I didn't see Marc or the kids for two weeks. They had no phone, and there was no way to get in touch with them. When I returned early from my trip, I went to Janelle's school and waited for her. She was still so thin, and her dark hair lacked the luster that every child's should have when properly nourished.

"Hi kiddo!"

"Candace!"

She ran to me, and hugged me tightly.

"How have you been?"

51

Her eyes looked down at the ground.

"Good, I guess."

"What's wrong?"

"Nothing."

"Come on; you can tell me."

Her head came up at me, and tears were in her eyes.

I stopped and knelt down to her. "What is it? Tell me."

"Our church is going to sing at City Hall next week. The thing is. . . ." The girl faltered, biting back tears. "They want us to wear a blue skirt and a white blouse. I don't have them. We can't afford it. Dad went to Pastor Cronin, and asked him if I could stand in the back, but he said that we'd have to march down the aisle, and everyone would see me. My heart went out to the girl. All that over a silly outfit.

"Come on."

I took her hand, and pulled her along the street.

We went into a local apparel shop where I purchased a simple white blouse and dark blue skirt for her—forcing myself into not buying her more things I knew she badly needed. The cashier handed Janelle the flowered shopping bag. She couldn't stop smiling and thanking me.

"You go on home, and I'll see you all soon."

She waved to me and went happily down the street.

It was 10:30 p.m. when I heard the loud banging on my front door. Alarmed, I looked through the small peephole opening. It was Marc. I opened the door, and he threw the flowered shopping bag at me.

"What the hell do you think you're doing?"

I was astonished.

"It's only a blouse and a skirt, the whole thing cost less than twenty dollars."

"Have you any idea what that amount of money means to people like us, Candace? You know how much it would buy if I shop carefully? Hell, you should; you've paid for my groceries before."

My face was aflame at the now insignificant memory.

"Why don't you come in, Marc, so we can talk about this."

I tried to urge him inside.

"There's nothing to talk about. Janelle has to learn that things are hard right now, and she can't have everything she wants, and she damn sure better not come running to you for anything!"

"Is that what you think she did? Marc she needs this for her concert next week, and I wanted to do it."

I shook the bag at him.

"We aren't taking anything from you. We don't need your charity, so you just stay away from my kids."

He stalked angrily away.

Perhaps Marc was right. Maybe I should just leave them alone, but my heart was telling me something else. I loved those kids, and every time I thought of him, I had a queer but pleasant feeling deep in my stomach.

I thought it best to give him some time to cool down.

As I fell into an uneasy sleep that night, I heard the sound of far-off sirens as they blared into oblivion.

So many times, I wanted to go by their place, but I didn't dare. Marc had been so angry, and seeing me, might've just added fuel to it. I forced myself to work late hours, so that I wouldn't go by Janelle's school or wait and watch James play during recess.

A month had passed, and I could not think of anything but Marc and the children. I had made up my mind, and I didn't care what happened. I was going to their house after work. On the way, I stopped at a bakery and got some cookies and a small cake—in an effort to make my visit a little more palatable. As I approached the street where they lived, I almost dropped the pastry box when I saw plank boards across the windows and front door of their building. The acrid smell of dead smoke assailed my nostrils. The charred ruins of what appeared to have been a terrible fire was all that remained. A man came outside the house next door, with an old mangy, rheumy-eyed dog.

"Sir . . . please . . . excuse me, but can you tell me what happened here?" I asked stupidly.

"Fire."

He moved on as I ran to catch up with him again.

"The people—where did they go?"

He looked at me as though I were mad.

"Nobody knows. Try the Red Cross; they were here."

The Red Cross! Of course.

I raced home and called the local chapter—only to be told that I would have to come down and make my inquiry in person during normal business hours—which were nine to five, Monday through Friday. I took off from work the next day, and went straight to The Red Cross office. It was futile. There was no record of Marc Hudson or his family. Even as she said it, my mind was racing, and another idea came to me. I went to Janelle's school. The principal sadly informed me that Janelle had not returned to school, and there had been no requests for a transfer of her records. I left the building sad and heartbroken. They were gone!

My mundane life had returned—except now, I spent much of my free time at the food kitchen hoping to once again fill an empty void. I guess I felt closest to Marc and the kids, there. Bojo talked me into other volunteer services. Soon, I found myself running to and from

53

various organizations—from the Rape Crisis Center to the Women's Abuse hotline. It was exhausting work, but fulfilling, and it helped to ease my loneliness and pain.

It was a hot August day, and I'd taken to getting off the bus five blocks from where I lived for some added exercise. I picked up my mail—consisting of magazines and bills—always bills. I thumbed through them, and stopped dead. A white envelope with a name and return address flashed up at me. Marc Hudson 173 Maynard Lane, Greenville SC. I stared at it for what seemed like an eternity. I went inside and sat down. I turned the envelope over and over in my hand. It was thin. Well! He certainly didn't have much to say. What explanation could he offer me as to why he took his kids and left, without a word for more than six months?

I don't care what he had to say; I wouldn't read it.

Oh! Who was I fooling? I picked up the envelope and tore it open.

My Dearest Candace,

I never thought I would ever want to fall in love, again, but I did. I've been in love with you almost from the first day I saw you. All I can give you is all I have. Speaking of which, I have a new job, a newer car—but the same kids. We're outside waiting to hear one word—which I hope is Yes!

Marc

Outside? Right now? I ran to the door and downstairs. There they were, fresh-faced and smiling. Janelle had filled out, and James was missing his two front teeth. Marc leaned against a sedan, the most horrible blue I'd ever seen. The kids scrambled to open the car door, and ran right into my open arms. Through my tears I looked at Marc who mouthed the words, "I love you."

That night, after dinner, when the kids were in bed. Marc told me about the fire. Someone had used a kerosene heater, and it was believed that it was what had caused the blaze. The old building caught up instantly. It happened so fast that all he was able to grab was the kids, a blanket, and his wallet. He hadn't bothered with the Red Cross—he just put the kids in the car, and began to drive.

"I didn't know where I was going, Candace. I just drove. But you know what I found out?"

I was filled with happiness just having him near me.

"What?" I asked, softly.

"There's so much kindness out in the world when you truly need it. I kept driving south, working for food and gas when I could. Many kind people let us stay the night in spare rooms, and they offered us sacks of food for our journey. But by the time I reached Greenville, I was flat broke, tired, and hungry."

54

He said he'd looked at his exhausted kids and knew that it was then or never. He had to do something—for them.

"I stopped at a diner, and with my last crumpled dollar, I bought a container of soup for Janelle and James. The owner, a massive woman well over three hundred pounds, followed me outside and when she saw the kids, she told me to bring them in."

After filling them with all the food they could eat, she asked him if he was looking for work and what he could do.

Not expecting her to understand, he told her. She surprised him by telling him that her son worked with "them puters."

"Grace, that was her name, and she called her son that very day. The next thing I knew, I had an interview."

"What about the kids?"

"I left them with her. Somehow, I knew I could trust her. Two hours later, I had a job."

Grace, and her husband, Joe, offered them a place in her house until he was on his feet.

"It's taken some time, Candace, but I found a new home, new friends, and a new church. There's only one thing missing: You."

"Me? But I. . . ."

"I know you care for me, and there's just no way I can't have you in my life, Candace. This is right. You feel it as well as I do."

He was right. We'd managed to fall in love without him even giving me a kiss. Well, at least not until that night.

Marc and I were married three weeks later in the church where I had first heard Janelle sing. I quit my job, and moved to Greenville with my family. Our lives are perfect. He is perfect, and his love for me is faultless.

I'm thankful everyday for this wonderful man and our kids—including the new baby girl I now carry—whom I will name Krystal Grace.

THE END

A DATE FOR THANKSGIVING
Honesty Is The Best Policy!

"**I** think you need to get over here so we can discuss what you're bringing for Thanksgiving," my sister said bossily.

"I always bring the green bean casserole, Amelia. What's to discuss?"

There was a pause and I could almost hear the cogs in my baby sister's brain turning as she tried to come up with something.

"Look, I'm not interested in meeting any of your friends," I said. "No matter how nice or pretty or wonderful they are."

"Well, you'll be glad to hear I don't have anyone left for you to meet!" Amelia snapped. "You've chased all of my friends away with your lousy attitude!"

"Sorry about that." I grinned.

"But there is something important I want to say to you," she admitted. "Please, Kenny."

I've never been very good at saying no to her and ten minutes later I was pulling into her driveway, wondering what it could be about. Thomas, my brother-in-law, was out of town on business so maybe my sister was just feeling a little lonely, but I had a feeling there was something more to it.

I grinned as the front door opened and my two nieces, Lara and Louise, ran out to say hi. They were wearing matching pink pajamas and I scooped them up in my arms to hurry them back inside. With Thanksgiving just two weeks away, the night was chilly. They were giggling as I kicked the door shut and set them down.

"Did you bring us some candy, Uncle Kenny?" four-year-old Louise asked me cheekily.

"That's rude!" six-year-old Lara said. "Anyway, we just brushed our teeth."

"I didn't bring candy, but how about if I read your bedtime story tonight?"

The girls nodded eagerly.

"Just a quick one," Amelia said, appearing in the kitchen doorway. "It's already late and I need to talk with your uncle."

I read the girls their favorite story. It wasn't particularly short, despite my sister's instructions. I didn't mind. I love hanging out with my nieces.

Louise was already asleep by the time I reached the end of the story and Lara was yawning. I bent down and kissed her, then switched off the pink lamp.

"'Night, Uncle Kenny," she whispered sleepily.

Amelia was still in the kitchen, tidying up.

"Have you eaten?" she quizzed me.

"I had a sandwich when I got home," I said.

My sister frowned, and then began rummaging in the fridge. "A sandwich isn't a proper meal," she scolded as she began heating up some leftovers.

A few minutes later I was obediently tucking into a plate of chicken and rice. Amelia was right. A sandwich isn't a proper meal. I'd never really mastered the art of cooking and it seemed so pointless anyway when you're on your own.

"What did you want to talk about?" I asked, in between bites.

Amelia hesitated. "Have you been watching much television lately?"

"A bit." I looked at her questioningly.

"Have you seen the ads for that new online dating service?" she asked.

Suddenly, I didn't like where the conversation was going. I stopped eating and pushed my plate away.

"I've signed you up for six months," Amelia said. "Think of it as an early Christmas present."

I scowled.

"I had to fill in a lot of details about your personality, interests, and so on," she continued. "It wasn't much trouble. I know you pretty well."

"Well, you can just go right ahead and unsign me. The last thing I want to do is join some stupid dating service!"

"It's not stupid!" Amelia protested.

"You had me come here under false pretences!" I said. "You said this had nothing to do with my love life!"

"No, I said I wasn't going to make you meet another one of my friends," Amelia corrected me.

"I'm not having any part of this. Why can't you just let all this drop, Amelia?"

She stared down in silence for a few moments before speaking. "Because of Sarah," she said quietly.

"Don't."

Amelia took the seat opposite me and gently touched my hand. "We hung out a lot together while Sarah was in the hospital. We did a lot of talking."

I sighed, wishing I were at home and not having this conversation. "I have to go now," I said, standing up.

"Look, do this one thing for me and I'll get off your back forever," Amelia pleaded.

I turned and looked at her.

"Go on one date," Amelia said. "One date. That's all I ask. If it doesn't work out, I'll never bug you again."

"Is that a promise?" It sounded too good to be true.

My sister nodded and I left the house without another word.

As I drove home, clouds covered the moon and it began to rain. I muttered a curse, gripping the steering wheel tightly. Why can't my family just leave this alone?

It had been three years since Sarah died and I had no intention of looking for someone else to settle down with, not now or ever. Amelia refused to accept that. She still believes in happy endings.

I knew I'd never find what I had with Sarah again, and it was pointless to even try. My wife had been perfect as far as I was concerned—a sweet, smart, kind-hearted woman who just happened to be incredibly beautiful. She'd been my lover, my best friend, and my everything before illness took her away. I just didn't want anyone else, not even after all this time.

I let myself into my apartment and headed straight for the shower, still thinking of Sarah. It came as no surprise to me that my wife had told Amelia she would want me to find someone else. Sarah had told me the same thing.

"Stop it," I'd said. "I don't want to hear that kind of talk."

"I'm trying to be practical," Sarah persisted. "Honey, I don't want you to be alone for the rest of your life."

That wasn't what I wanted, either. The trouble was, the only person I wanted was Sarah, and that's no longer possible.

I rarely bothered checking my email, but after my shower I switched on my computer. Sighing, I saw that the website had contacted me, welcoming me to their online community of hopeful singles. For the next six months I would have access to their forums and a host of other activities. Meanwhile, they'd forwarded my email address to six compatible members.

With another sigh, I began to open emails from women who wanted to date me. Unimpressed, I read about hobbies and hopes for the future. Then I decided on one completely at random and clicked reply. Amelia had told me she'd get off my back if I went on one date, so the sooner I got it over with the better.

I clicked open the attached picture of Kelly, the woman whose letter I'd decided to answer, without much interest. Suddenly, a woman in her early thirties was looking at me from the screen with a shy smile. A tabby cat sat on her lap.

Dear Kelly, I wrote. My name is Kenny Powers and I'm a single guy of thirty-four. I enjoy long walks, eating out, and reading. Would you like to meet? Kenny.

I hit send, thinking I sounded as boring as Kelly would think.

I really don't want to be doing this, I thought, with a feeling of sadness and guilt. Kelly looked like a nice lady and she had every right to go after her dream of meeting a decent guy and settling down. I frowned, wishing Amelia hadn't put me in that position, suddenly regretting that I'd emailed Kelly.

But it was too late for regrets. I received a brief reply minutes later. Hi, Kenny! I'd love to meet. What kind of food do you like? Kelly.

We arranged to meet up the following evening at a nearby restaurant. I couldn't sleep that night. Meeting Kelly, meeting any woman, in a restaurant was the last thing I wanted to do. What on earth would we talk about? I didn't have anything interesting to say. I'm just a guy who works in construction. Despite what I'd told her, I rarely ate out, and I read maybe one or two books a year. What will I say to Kelly? How will we get through this evening?

I pulled on a fresh shirt that night and I hoped she'd find me so boring she'd never want to set eyes on me again. That way I wouldn't have to feel so bad.

When I arrived at the restaurant to find Kelly hadn't gotten there yet, my hopes raised a notch. Maybe I've been stood up! I sipped water and glanced at my watch for ten minutes before I realized someone was approaching. Reluctantly, I looked up. My first thought was that Kelly was prettier than her picture. I noticed she walked with a slight limp.

Forcing a smile, I stood up.

"Hello. You must be Kelly."

"Hello, Kenny," she said, shyly. "I'm sorry I'm late. One of my cats is sick."

"That's okay," I replied as we sat down. Ordering our food took a few minutes, and then we were alone. An awkward silence descended.

"So," Kelly said. "Where do you live?'

For the next several minutes we exchanged small talk about our homes. When our food arrived, we both began to eat hungrily. I liked the way Kelly seemed to be a hearty eater. I couldn't stand it when women just nibbled at their food.

"What?" she asked, looking at me as I grinned.

"I just like the way you're enjoying your food," I said.

"Not very ladylike, am I?"

Our eyes met and some of the tension between us melted. I felt a tug of affection, and I knew I needed to tell her the truth as quickly as possible. I didn't want to string her along all evening, and then tell her I didn't think we'd hit it off. She deserved better.

I took a sip of water and laid down my fork. "Listen, Kelly. There's something I need to say."

Her big, gray eyes looked into mine. "Yes?"

Why is this so difficult? "I, um, I mean I'm only on this date because I promised my sister I'd. . . ."

"Kenny." Those eyes of hers seemed to look deep into my soul. "It's okay," she said softly. "I know that after tonight we'll never see each other again. I guessed that the moment I saw you."

I frowned. "How?"

"Let's be realistic here." She smiled. "You're a tall, drop-dead gorgeous guy. I'm the type men don't give a second glance. Plain in appearance, I limp; I'm completely average in every way. We're hardly a match made in heaven. Maybe the matchmaking computers have a glitch!"

I shook my head as she giggled. "You're not average. You're beautiful."

She waved at me with her napkin, turning pink. "Oh, stop it!"

"You are," I said seriously. "Your looks, and the fact that you walk with a slight limp, have nothing to do with what I said. You see, my wife died and I just . . . I can't do this."

"I understand," she said softly. "Let's just relax and enjoy the rest of our meal, shall we?"

The conversation seemed to clear the air, and relax was exactly what we did. I learned a lot about Kelly that evening. Her limp was the result of a car accident she'd been in at the age of nine, which had killed both her parents. An aunt and uncle already busy raising a bunch of her cousins had raised her. Years later, just after graduating college, she'd fallen in love with a man she described as "wonderful." He left her after seven years, wanting to pursue his career abroad without a wife.

Kelly shrugged. "Maybe it was for the best. I don't think I'd have been happy so far away from home."

"So you're hoping to find someone who wants the same things as you?" I asked gently.

She nodded. "For a long time I thought I never would. Now I'm not so sure. I think I've got a lot to offer somebody out there, if I can ever find him!"

"I know you will," I said. "You certainly deserve to."

"What about you?" Kelly asked. "Surely there'll come a time when you'll feel the need to settle down again?"

"Maybe." I shrugged. "But what I had with my wife was pretty amazing. You don't find that twice in a lifetime."

"You're so lucky, Kenny," she said.

I stared at her. "Lucky? How'd you figure that?"

"I'd give anything to find my once in a lifetime love."

I nodded slowly. "I guess I was pretty lucky."

Our conversation drifted along to other subjects easily. I found myself telling Kelly about the house I'd always wanted to build, the log cabin with mountain views and a wraparound deck. We laughed together about a comedy show we both loved. By the time we'd finished dessert and the waiter brought our bill, I realized I'd been enjoying myself. It was the last thing I'd expected.

As we left the restaurant I wondered if I should ask Kelly if I could see her again, just as a friend. But I bit my lip and said nothing. Kelly didn't join a dating service looking for friendship. It would be wrong of me to waste her time.

"Thank you for a lovely evening, Kenny," she said as we left the restaurant.

"You're welcome." I shoved my hands deep into the pockets of my jacket. It was a chilly night and the air smelled of wood smoke. I imagined couples sitting together by the fire. I wondered suddenly how that would feel with Kelly, how it would feel to hold her in my arms as we laughed and talked. "Can I walk you to your car?" I asked.

She shook her head. "No. It's just across the street."

"Well, I hope you find everything you're looking for."

"I hope you do, too," she replied, and then surprised me by brushing a soft, quick kiss on my cheek. "Bye."

Depression settled over me as I drove home. I wasn't sure why. I'd just enjoyed a great evening with a beautiful, funny woman. I was honest with her about my feelings and she'd accepted the situation straight away. So why did I feel as if I'd just lost something very precious?

As I tried to fall asleep that night I told myself I was just a little confused. It had been so long since I'd enjoyed being around a woman and my mind didn't know how to deal with it. Being honest with Kelly was the right thing to do, I told myself firmly. She's a wonderful woman, but she isn't my type—even if I did want a relationship.

The phone rang the following morning before I'd been out of bed ten minutes.

"So, how did it go?" Amelia asked, not even bothering to wish me a good morning.

I sighed. "It was fine."

"Fine? What does that mean?" my sister demanded.

"It means I had a good time," I admitted reluctantly.

"You did? Oh, that's fantastic!" Amelia sounded thrilled. "What was she like? What was her name?"

"She was very nice and her name's Kelly," I replied.

"And? When are you seeing her again?" Amelia asked.

"I'm not."

There was a long silence. "But you just said you had a good time," Amelia said.

"I did! But I'm not ready for anything long-term," I said. "Not with anyone."

Amelia sighed. "Okay, Kenny."

After we said good-bye I forced myself to start getting on with my day, instead of sitting around thinking of Kelly. Sunday was my day for doing housework, reading the paper, and listening to music. I turned the music up loud while I scrubbed the bathtub and vacuumed. It didn't do any good.

I couldn't chase away the memory of Kelly's smile no matter how hard I tried. It rarely left her face as she talked. It was infectious, making me smile and relax. Kelly's life hadn't exactly been a picnic, yet she saw the good in everything, refusing to give up hope. She's brave, I thought. Much braver than me.

As I pulled the vacuum cleaner plug from the wall, something toppled from the shelf by the television. I picked up the framed picture of Sarah and stared at it for several moments. My wife was a glowingly beautiful woman with long, blond hair and a movie-star smile. She'd owned a small fashion boutique and loved glamorous clothes.

Sarah and Kelly appeared so different on the surface, yet they're so similar. Sarah saw humor in every situation, too. She was funny and full of kindness, tackling every challenge that came her way with courage—including cancer.

"You'd like Kelly, sweetheart," I murmured to the photograph.

I worked hard the following week, still trying to banish thoughts of Kelly. I found myself wondering how she was doing at the dating service. Had she found anyone special yet? It surely wouldn't take long for some lucky guy to realize how wonderful she was. The thought made me feel oddly jealous.

Even hanging out with Lara and Louise at my sister's house didn't make me feel any better. Two days before Thanksgiving, Amelia was all ready for the big day. Her house smelled of freshly baked cookies and peach cobbler. While she sat at the dining room table making a list, the girls played in front of a crackling fire with Thomas.

Amelia chewed the end of her pencil thoughtfully.

"We're going to have a full house this year. Mom and Dad are bringing over a couple of their friends. Kenny, do you think you could bake an extra pie?"

"Sure," I said.

"Could you make it apple?" she asked, then quickly shook her head. "No, forget I said that. Another pumpkin pie, please, and I'll try to remember some extra whipped cream."

"Whatever." I shrugged.

My sister looked at me. "I sure hope you're in a better mood by Thanksgiving."

"Maybe I should just stay home. Would that suit you?" I snapped.

"You know, I think it just might!" Amelia shot back.

I stood up and walked out. As I shrugged into my jacket, Thomas caught up with me in the hallway.

"Hold on, Kenny," he said quietly.

Everyone in the family had been amazed when Amelia brought Thomas home after announcing she was madly in love. I guess we were all expecting a flashy extrovert, full of ideas and chatter like Amelia. Thomas is a quiet, steady, sensible man. Somehow he and my sister complement each other perfectly.

"Why don't you just give her a call?" he suggested.

I frowned, feeling my face flush. "What're you talking about?"

"Oh, come on." He smiled gently. "You've been like a bear with a sore head ever since that date you went on last week."

I sighed. There was no point in denying it.

"She got under your skin, didn't she?" Thomas persisted.

"I guess," I admitted reluctantly. "I'm not sure calling her would be the right thing to do, Thom. I don't know if I'm over Sarah. I don't know if I can give Kelly what she's looking for. . . ." I trailed off, shaking my head.

"There's always a lot of uncertainty at the beginning of a relationship," Thomas pointed out. "You never know where things might lead. You just have to have the courage to start the journey."

I nodded slowly. That was a part of it. I was scared. The last time I gave a woman my heart, she died. I wasn't sure I had the courage to risk loving and losing all over again.

I must have picked up the phone only to set it down again a hundred times that evening. Finally, with grim determination, I dialed Kelly's number. I felt a moment of panic when she picked up, as I wondered what to say.

"Um, hi. It's me, Kenny," I stuttered, feeling stupid as I tried to sound casual. "I just wondered how you were doing."

She was silent for a moment. "Oh. Hey, Kenny."

I swallowed. She didn't sound particularly pleased to hear from me.

"I won't keep you," I said. "You're probably busy getting ready for Thanksgiving. I was just thinking of you."

"That's sweet. I'm doing okay, thanks."

"Are you meeting lots of people?" I asked.

"You mean through the website?" Kelly sighed. "Not exactly."

"Did you give up your membership?"

"No. It's just that. . . ." Kelly sighed again. "Let's face it. Most men aren't looking for a plain-faced woman with a limp, which is what I am."

"What are you talking about?" I demanded, annoyed. She shouldn't be describing herself in such a negative way! "There are a bunch of men out there who'd love to be with you!"

Kelly laughed with a touch of sadness. "Maybe you could give me their names! So far I've had six very pleasant dates with men who explain that they think I'm very nice, but they never want to see me again."

"Then they're crazy!" I said.

Kelly laughed. "You and I had exactly one date, and actually I appreciated your honesty when you told me how you felt."

I flushed at the reminder. "That was different, though. It was because of losing my wife. It had nothing to do with you."

"Well, I've decided to give up dating for a while," Kelly said. "If I'm meant to meet somebody, it'll happen."

"The reason I called was to ask if we could get together again for dinner. We seemed to hit it off and I'd really like to see you again."

There was such a long silence I began to sweat. Then Kelly spoke. "No, thanks."

I swallowed back my disappointment.

"You don't have to feel sorry for me, Kenny," Kelly added gently. "Happy Thanksgiving."

She hung up and I was left holding the phone, my mouth open in astonishment. Sorry for her? She couldn't have been more wrong! Maybe those other guys had been too dumb to appreciate Kelly for the lovely woman she is, but that certainly wasn't my problem!

I dialed her number again, and when she picked up the phone I launched into my speech.

"Listen. I think you're a beautiful, funny, wonderful woman. The reason I haven't asked you for a second date before now is that I've been scared. You see, the last time I cared for a woman I ended up losing her. But I've been accused of acting like a bear with a sore head since last week, and that happens to be all your fault. I can't get you out of my mind, Kelly. That's why I want to see you again."

"Oh, Kenny," she said softly.

"I know it's short notice, but how about tonight?"

There was a short pause. "Alright," she said.

I don't believe in love at first sight. I never have, but when Kelly walked into the café where we'd arranged to meet, I had the oddest feeling. It was as if a part of my soul that'd been missing for a long time had finally found its way back home.

She smiled and my heart stood still. She looked so pretty in jeans and a denim shirt, her curly hair framing her sweet face.

We'd talked about anything and everything on our first date, but kept things pretty lighthearted. That night I found myself telling

64

Kelly about Sarah, about the raw pain I'd suffered, the hole of grief I wondered if I'd ever be able to climb out of. Kelly told me about her loneliness. About being adopted by a family but always feeling like an outsider, and hoping that she wasn't destined to always feel that way.

"Do you have plans for Thanksgiving?" I asked.

She hesitated. "Kenny, I don't want your family stuck with a surprise guest at the last minute!"

"Are you kidding? My sister would be thrilled if I brought a guest!" I smiled.

All of a sudden Kelly looked nervous and vulnerable. "I don't know if I'm ready to meet your family."

I reached across the small table and took her hands in mine. "Please," I said softly. "I'd love to spend the holiday with you."

Her eyes widened, and then she nodded.

My family can be more than a little overwhelming and I felt a little nervous myself the following afternoon when I turned up at Amelia's house with Kelly. I shouldn't have been. Kelly took everything in her stride—the sticky hugs from Lara and Louise, the talk from Amelia that made me sound like the bachelor of the year, the noise, and all the nosy questions.

One of the Thanksgiving traditions we have in our family is that during dinner, everyone would take a turn to say what they were thankful for. It was something I had trouble with since losing Sarah, but I managed a smile as I squeezed Kelly's fingers under the table. I was finally starting to believe there might be a way out of the hole of grief after all.

Just as we were about to leave, Amelia pulled me to one side.

"Kenny, she's lovely!"

I couldn't keep the smile off my face. I dropped Kelly off at her apartment, walking her through the chilly evening to her front door. Swirls of golden leaves fluttered around our feet as I realized I didn't want to say good-bye.

Kelly looked up at me as we reached her door.

"I had such a wonderful time," she said. "Thank you."

"Can we get together again soon?" I asked.

"I'd like that," she replied, her voice shy.

Then we stood gazing awkwardly at each other. Never in my life had I wanted to kiss a woman so badly. A leaf caught in Kelly's hair suddenly and I gently removed it, then bent and touched my lips to hers. She responded immediately, kissing me back with a sweet longing that took my breath away.

I was still floating on air when I reached home. Knowing I wouldn't be able to pay it any attention, I switched on the television, and then grinned. An ad for the online dating service was playing. I'd always found it annoying in the past, but now I smiled at the image of a couple walking along hand-in-hand as a voiceover asked, "Why don't you take a chance? Maybe you'll find your forever love the way thousands of our happy customers already have!"

Suddenly, I felt so thankful that I'd taken a chance; that I'd found the courage to call Kelly and tell her what was in my heart. One year on, another Thanksgiving holiday has arrived. There will be the same family favorites—a green bean casserole and pumpkin pie, buttery dinner rolls, and a plump, golden turkey. However, one thing has changed. The sprit of thankful joy lives in my heart these days.

Kelly, my wife to be, will be at my side. The past twelve months have been a journey for us both, leading to a deeper love. This year, when it's my turn to say what I'm thankful for, it's going to be a cinch!

THE END

A THANKSGIVING TO REMEMBER
We may not have enjoyed the traditional harvest feast
at home, but what we did have was so much more. . . .

"I'm sorry about ruining your Thanksgiving," I said to Brad
as we pulled into the parking lot of St. Mary's Hospital. "Still, there's
no reason why you can't just drop me off here and go on to dinner at
your parents'."

He shook his head. "I planned to spend my Thanksgiving with
you. Besides, I wouldn't feel right leaving you when your mother's
having a heart attack."

Brad's determination to be by my side was heartwarming. I
thought for the thousandth time how lucky I was to have him in my
life. He was the kindest and most considerate man I'd ever met. For
instance, he wanted to be with me at the hospital even though he'd
never met my mother.

Brad and I were talking and laughing as we left my apartment to
go to his parents' house when the telephone rang. I was surprised to hear
Carl Blackwell, one of Mom's neighbors, on the line. I hadn't talked to
him in years and it took me a minute to realize who was on the phone.
Carl's words tumbled out as he explained that Mom had experienced
chest pains and had trouble breathing after her morning jog. The
paramedics said that she was having a heart attack, so they were taking
her to St. Mary's Hospital. The news was totally unexpected because
Mom was in excellent health and had never had heart trouble.

As Brad drove us to the hospital, I tried to remember the last time
I'd talked to Mom. At least a month had gone by since she'd called
me to see how I was doing. As usual, our conversation had been short
and impersonal. Since last Thanksgiving, I seldom saw or talked to
her. I didn't know how to talk to her anymore. She was no longer the
person I'd thought she was. She was a phony—a person whom I no
longer believed or trusted.

All of my life, Mom had been like a best friend to me. When I
was going to school I'd easily shared all my adolescent worries and
fears with her and she'd always had a ready answer to help me. She'd
helped me with my boyfriend and dating troubles, and was a great
source of advice about boys. She was a good role model as a wife,
too; she and Dad were the happiest married couple I knew. They never
fought or argued like a lot of my friends' parents did. But then last
Thanksgiving, Mom had made an announcement that changed Dad's
life and my life forever.

We'd just finished Thanksgiving dinner and I was looking around the table at my parents' faces. My heart warmed as I realized just how lucky I was to be so close to my parents and to come from a happy home. Even though I was an only child, I'd never missed having brothers and sisters because my family life was so fulfilling. Then my gaze rested on Mom's face and I looked twice at what I saw. There were tears in her eyes and her composure was cracking.

After several minutes of confused conversation where Dad and I tried to find out what was wrong with Mom, she told us that she was a lesbian. She'd tried to ignore her feelings for years, but recently she'd begun a relationship with Samantha, my parents' next-door neighbor. With Samantha, Mom's life was filled with a happiness that she'd never felt before.

I have no problem accepting that people are gays or lesbians. But accepting that my mother was a lesbian while pretending to be happily married to my dad all those years was impossible. She'd been terribly dishonest to him. She'd been dishonest with me, too, with all of her comments about hoping that I would have a happy marriage like hers someday, and all the advice that she'd given me about attracting boys. She'd only been pretending to have a happy marriage. And what did she know about attracting boys? She didn't even like men. Everything I knew or thought I knew about her was a sham.

This year I'd planned a wonderful Thanksgiving weekend. On Thanksgiving Day, I was going to have dinner with Brad and his family while Dad had dinner with some of his friends. The next day, Brad and I were going to the Christmas tree lighting in the town square with Dad. Afterward, we were all going to dinner at our favorite restaurant nearby. It would be a perfect Thanksgiving—without Mom.

But it looks like I'll be spending Thanksgiving with Mom, after all, I thought, as Brad pulled the car into a parking spot and we climbed out.

I glanced at Brad, in his suit and black overcoat, as he walked with me toward the emergency entrance. Brad had come into my life a few months ago, when he started working in the network support unit at the county office where I design webpages. Brad stood out from the rest of the network group because he was single and very good looking. We were attracted to each other right away and I was overjoyed when he asked me to lunch one day. That first lunch date quickly turned into dinners and more.

Soon after we'd started dating, I'd introduced Brad to Dad, but I'd delayed having him meet Mom. I'd told Brad that Mom and I weren't that close and that someday I'd arrange a meeting when she wasn't too busy at her job. I didn't want to have to explain to Brad about Mom being a lesbian. I wasn't ashamed of her lifestyle; I was appalled by the dishonesty of her life and by how Dad and I had been fooled. I knew Brad was accepting of alternate lifestyles, but he was an honest person and I knew he'd have trouble accepting what Mom had done. Unfortunately, Samantha would be waiting for me at the hospital, so I wouldn't be able to stall explanations much longer.

Brad and I swept through the hospital's sliding glass doors and into the emergency room waiting area. I scanned the crowd of people in the waiting room, looking for Samantha, but I didn't see her.

"I'll talk to the nurse at the reception desk," I said, as Brad sat down in one of the few vacant chairs.

The nurse at the reception desk told me she'd check on my mother. I leaned against the counter and gazed down a corridor where two paramedics pushed a stretcher carrying a woman toward the treatment rooms. An IV bag swung from a pole attached to the stretcher, a heart monitor rested at the woman's feet, and oxygen poured into her nose through a canula. My blood ran cold thinking of Mom being rushed into the hospital like the woman on the stretcher. I didn't want Mom to die, but the more I thought about her dying, the more I realized that the part of her that I'd loved had died last year. She was now a woman whom I didn't trust and didn't really know.

The sliding doors opened and the nurse emerged. "Your mother has some blockage in her heart that caused her problems this morning. The blockages were fairly serious, so Dr. Hansen took her upstairs to see if he can clear them."

"So, I can't see her?"

The nurse pursed her lips in a sympathetic expression and shook her head. "No, I'm sorry. The procedure is already underway." She gave me an encouraging smile. "You should wait in the surgical waiting room on the fourth floor. Dr. Hansen will talk with you as soon as he's done with the procedure." Then the nurse gave me instructions on how to get to the waiting room.

"Let's go," Brad said as he put his arm around my shoulders. I was so involved in my conversation with the nurse that I hadn't realized he'd gotten up from his chair and joined me. I turned and met Brad's gaze—it warmed my heart and soul. He hugged me against him and led me toward the elevators.

"It's too bad you can't talk to your mother," Brad said as we got into the elevator.

"Unfortunately, talking with her isn't as easy as it used to be." I struggled to find the right words to explain. "Something happened, so we aren't as close now."

His eyes met mine. "You've mentioned that you're not close anymore and I've wondered about it. You and your dad have such a good relationship."

"It's a complicated story."

"You don't have to talk about it. Right now, we need to find the waiting room."

Samantha was the only person in the waiting room. She was sitting on the edge of a sofa with her gaze fixed on a set of double doors marked: Operating Rooms—Authorized Staff Only. I was struck by her messy appearance. Usually, Samantha was stylishly dressed, her hair and makeup perfect. Now, her face was pale without makeup, her hair was a mess, and she was wearing jogging pants and a faded sweatshirt. She bounded out of her chair when she saw us.

"Thank God you're here." She clasped both of my hands in hers and held them tightly. "We were on our morning run and your mother was having trouble keeping up. We thought it was because she'd just gotten over a cold," Samantha babbled as she explained what had happened. "When we got home, Bobbi had to sit down because her chest hurt. Then she couldn't breathe. I called the paramedics right away."

"I'm sure you did everything you could." I steered her back to the sofa. Her body was shaky and panic filled her eyes.

"Bobbi never had heart trouble. She jogs every day." Samantha rattled on about Mom's good health and then her gaze met Brad's. "I'm sorry; we don't know each other. I'm Samantha Madison." She held out her hand to Brad.

"This is Brad Sheppard," I said as they shook hands.

The introductions seemed to break Samantha's panicky mood. She sighed and leaned back against the sofa cushions. She talked about Mom's cold and how Mom had been slow to get her energy back. We were discussing how Mom was the most energetic person we knew when the double doors opened and a doctor dressed in blue-green scrubs walked into the room.

After brief introductions, he sat down on the edge of the coffee table so he could see all of us. "Bobbi's blockages are too complicated to clear with simple procedures, so she's on her way to the operating room for bypass surgery."

Samantha bit her lip and tears filled her eyes. Dr. Hansen gave Samantha's hand a soft squeeze, and then he explained the procedure and how he was confident that Mom would do well. I'd never met Dr. Hansen before, but I felt confident listening to him explain his credentials and the surgery. It was clear that he was an experienced heart surgeon and was very familiar with the operation he was going to perform on Mom.

Dr. Hansen pushed himself off the coffee table and stood up. He glanced at the clock on the wall. "I should be done with her surgery around five o'clock," he said. "I'll talk with you as soon as I'm done."

I watched him as he left the room. The three of us talked for a few minutes about the surgery and how we thought that Dr. Hansen was very qualified to perform the procedure. It was going to be a long wait and I knew that Brad probably hadn't eaten anything since breakfast. Dr. Hansen had said it would take a while to prep Mom for surgery, so I knew she wasn't in surgery yet. This would be a good time to get something to eat in the cafeteria.

"I'll stay here," Samantha said when I asked if she wanted to come.

"Would you like us to bring you back something?"

Samantha shook her head at first, but then she changed her mind and asked for a sandwich. "I can get a drink here." She pointed to the vending machine that sold pop and other drinks.

Being around Samantha was a strain for me and was adding to the tension that was making my neck and head ache. I'd often talked to her since she was my parents' neighbor. She and I liked to read the same novels and we'd always had lively conversations about books, authors, and movies. But after she and Mom became a couple, I didn't talk with her much. I felt awkward around her now. I wasn't used to thinking of her as Mom's lover.

Even though I'd eaten only a light breakfast hours ago, I wasn't hungry. But I wanted Brad to have the opportunity to eat and I needed some space away from Samantha. "It's going to be a long wait," I said to Brad as we walked toward the cafeteria. "Why don't you go to your parents' and enjoy the rest of the day with them?"

"I called Mom when you stopped in the restroom and I told her that we'd have Thanksgiving leftovers with her on Saturday. Mom and Dad understand completely that we need to be here today."

I smiled at Brad and thought again that I was lucky to have him in my life. He was so caring and kind. We walked through the cafeteria line, got light snacks, and I also selected a tuna sandwich to take back to Samantha. We found a table near a window and sat down. I was trying to find the best way to tell Brad about Mom and Samantha. I always had difficulty talking about the situation. Even my best friend, Becky, had been taken aback when I told her.

"How could you not know that she was a lesbian?" Becky had asked. "You lived with her." From there the conversation had been painful, and I was left feeling even more alienated from my mother. Mom had been a good actress for all of those years.

"It's a good thing Samantha was with your mom this morning," Brad said as he unwrapped his sandwich. "She sounds like a good friend."

Samantha hadn't said or done anything that would cause Brad to believe she was more than just Mom's friend. "Samantha is more than a friend to Mom," I began.

"Oh?" He looked up from his tray. "She's her sister?"

"No, Samantha is Mom's partner."

71

At first Brad was confused and thought that I meant that Samantha was Mom's jogging partner. Then I explained about Mom's relationship to Samantha, and about how things had changed last Thanksgiving. Brad was so interested in what I said that he didn't touch his sandwich or Coke until I was done talking. Then I braced myself, waiting for him to ask me how come I'd never figured out that Mom was a lesbian, but he didn't ask that. His response surprised me.

"Your mother must've been unhappy for a long time."

"I suppose she was," I admitted. I'd never thought about how Mom had dealt with her feelings through the years. My concerns had been for my father and how he'd been deceived, and how I'd been fooled. "But what she did was so deceitful." I talked for several minutes about how my father must feel, knowing that his marriage was a sham, and how I felt.

"I can see how you might feel that way," Brad agreed. "It would be shocking to find that out after so many years. It sounds like you had a close relationship with her before this happened."

"Probably closer than most mothers and daughters. She was like my best friend."

"Maybe this medical crisis will bring the two of you back together again," he suggested. "Sometimes a crisis will do that."

"Maybe." But I didn't believe it.

We talked some more about Samantha, and how I'd also been closer to her. While Brad listened to me, he also kept talking about how Mom must have been unhappy for so long. He even thought life had to be difficult for Samantha now. But I kept thinking about Dad's feelings and mine.

I thought I was going to faint when Brad and I walked into the waiting room. Dad was sitting next to Samantha on the sofa.

"Dad. What are you doing here?"

Dad got up and hugged me. "Samantha called me about your mom."

I gathered my thoughts while Brad and Dad greeted each other. Then Dad made sure that Samantha had met Brad. What was Dad doing here? Why would he care about Mom? Samantha had called him? Why? None of this was making any sense.

"While you were in the cafeteria, a nurse came out and said that the surgery had started on schedule and that they expected to be done around five o'clock," Samantha said.

I glanced at the clock. We still had hours to wait. Brad and I sat down in chairs near Samantha and Dad. The four of us talked about the surgeon and the surgery. Then Dad turned to Brad and asked him about work. Dad explained to Samantha that Brad and I worked together at the county office. I was speechless as I watched Dad carry on a conversation with Samantha and Brad like he talked to Samantha every day. I wanted to ask Dad why he was there, but there was no way that I could do that.

The hours dragged. We shared stories about people we knew who'd had heart surgery, we talked about our jobs, and we discussed the latest political and economic topics. With Dad around it was easier to talk with Samantha. I still couldn't understand why he was there, though. Mom had ruined their marriage and hurt him deeply. I couldn't imagine that he'd be so concerned about her. Even if he was concerned, he could find out about her condition through a phone call. He didn't need to sit in a stuffy hospital waiting room with his ex-wife's new lesbian lover.

At a few minutes after five o'clock, the double doors opened and Dr. Hansen stepped out. His scrubs were damp with sweat and he was carrying a wadded-up surgical cap in one hand. "Things went well," he said. He smiled and discussed some of the details of Mom's surgery. "She'll be in the recovery room for some time before she's moved to the ICU." He explained that the ICU was on the seventh floor, and that we could expect to see her in about two hours. After Dr. Hansen left, we talked about the good news and how we liked the way Dr. Hansen had talked with us.

"How about dinner?" Dad suggested. "Everyone's got to be hungry by now."

"Sounds good to me," Brad said. I still wasn't hungry, but I knew Brad had only had a small sandwich hours ago.

"When I walked into the hospital, I saw a sign announcing that the cafeteria is serving Thanksgiving dinner tonight," Dad said. "It won't be as good as home cooking, but it will be a turkey dinner. And I'll buy." Dad got up from his chair and headed toward the hall. Brad and I were following closely behind him when Dad abruptly stopped and turned back. "Samantha, aren't you coming?" he called.

"I thought you might like to be together as a family," she said. Her voice was soft and hesitant.

I thought about some of the things that Brad had said about Samantha's feelings and I was filled with empathy for the position that she was in. "You come, too," I said. I smiled and our eyes met. Her eyes were glassy, as if she were fighting back tears. Tears because Mom was okay? Or because we wanted her to come to dinner with us?

Dad was correct about the Thanksgiving dinner. The cafeteria was serving roast turkey with all of the trimmings, including pumpkin pie with whipped cream. Although I was still confused about Dad's presence, I was so relived that Mom had come through the surgery that the food was beginning to look tasty to me. As we started through the cafeteria line, Dad reached his arm around my shoulders and hugged me against his chest. "We have lots to be thankful for, Chloe. Mom's going to be okay."

I wanted to ask why he was there, but I held my words because Samantha was standing beside us.

Like a thoughtful host, Dad selected a round table for us and made sure that everyone had silverware and napkins. I was still dumbfounded about the way he and Samantha talked together. I didn't expect him to be rude to her; my dad is never rude to anyone. But they talked like old friends.

The turkey dinner wasn't like a homemade one, but the food was flavorful and seemed like the perfect way to celebrate the hopeful feelings around the table. After we were done eating, Dad suggested that Brad and Samantha go up to the ICU. "I need to go outside and use my cell phone. Chloe can keep me company while I'm outside. There's a park right across the street from the hospital where we can go," he said as we walked out of the hospital.

I pulled my coat around my neck and buttoned it up. It was much colder out than it had been that morning. I was glad that Dad and I were alone because I wanted to ask him why he'd come, and why he was staying so long. We found a park bench that overlooked the hospital and sat down.

"I could see questions in your eyes today."

I wasted no time getting to the point. "I don't understand why you're here."

"I care about your mom and what happens to her."

"How can you care about her? She deceived you and ruined your marriage," I began. Dad was expressionless as he sat listening to me. If he wouldn't talk, I would. I kept on listing all the reasons that should keep him away. "Your marriage was a lie. Our whole life as a family was a lie." I talked on and on. Finally, I paused to see if he was listening to me.

"That's a lot of feelings," he said at last. "I've wondered what you thought about the situation. We've never really talked about it."

"There's nothing to talk about," I said.

"Yes, there is. Your relationship with your mother is a good place to start."

"She lied to me and she lied to you," I said. "I don't see how you can be so calm about it."

He gave a soft laugh. "I wasn't at first. I felt all the painful feelings that you described—probably more. But then I started looking at things differently. For years I'd felt that something wasn't right with my marriage. I was always blaming myself for a problem I couldn't even identify. Last Thanksgiving, I finally knew what had been wrong with my marriage. And it wasn't anything that I was doing."

"That's true," I agreed, not knowing what else to say. "But Mom still deceived us."

"Out of love," he said. "Your mother wanted us to be a happy family. She may not have loved me as a wife loves a husband, but she treated me with love. Over the years, she and I shared many of life's challenges together—and survived as a couple—not because of sex, but because we had a good relationship together."

I was embarrassed when he mentioned sex, and I was glad that the streetlights were dim so that he couldn't see me blush. He talked at length about how Mom had supported him through several job changes, and how he'd been there for her when her mom died of cancer. "As for the way she treated you, I've never seen a better mother," he said. He went on to talk about how Mom had always loved me and wanted me to be happy.

I gave a sarcastic laugh. "She always said she wanted me to have a marriage like hers," I said. "And she didn't even like her marriage."

"Chloe, you're making things worse than they are. Of course she'd say something like that because we had a traditional marriage, and most of our married life was good."

I had to admit that he was probably right; I was finding fault, rather than looking at the big picture and what Mom really meant.

"Your mother is one of the most courageous women that I know."

"She is?" I'd never looked at her that way.

"For years she put her feelings aside to make our lives happy. She also tried to change her internal feelings toward me, but couldn't. Finally, she had the courage to admit what would make her happy."

I thought about Brad's remark earlier—about how Mom's life must have been unhappy for a long time. The more I listened to Dad, the more I realized that Mom's life hadn't been easy—a life of quiet pain and longing. She may have also felt dishonest and guilty.

"Have you and Mom talked about this?"

"Yes, at great length—many, many times." His voice was soft and serious. "We're still friends and we talk frequently. Like I said, we had a good relationship—we just didn't have what it takes for a lasting marriage."

We sat quietly for a few minutes. I looked through the park at the hospital and thought about Mom being in there with both Samantha and Dad at her side.

"I know her admission last year was a surprise." Dad's voice interrupted my thoughts. "But we don't need to let it destroy our relationships with each other. We've always had a solid family foundation, and those feelings and bonds are still with us." He wrapped his arm around my shoulders. "Your mother is a special person; don't shut her out of your life because she tried to live a life that couldn't make her happy."

Dad and I found Brad and Samantha seated in a small waiting room near the doors to the ICU. Brad was telling her about some of the projects we'd worked on together. I slipped into the chair next to him as Dad took

75

a seat next to Samantha. We'd barely sat down when a nurse came into the room.

"We've got Bobbi settled in her room," she explained. "She's sedated and on a ventilator. You can come back for a few minutes to see her, but she won't know you're there."

Brad said he'd wait in the waiting room while Dad, Samantha, and I went to see Mom.

I'd never seen anyone after a major operation—or on a ventilator. At the first sight of Mom, I reached for Dad's hand. A plastic tube in Mom's mouth was attached to the ventilator; IV lines flowed in both of her arms and electrodes from her chest led to a heart monitor, and her chest rhythmically went up and down with each click of the ventilator. She was pasty white and looked more like a store mannequin than a human being.

"I know she looks uncomfortable," the nurse said, "but she's heavily sedated and in no pain. We'll remove the breathing tube around midnight, and then she'll be breathing on her own."

I stood holding Dad's hand as I gazed down at Mom. For the first time, I wondered what psychological pains she'd had as she tried to make her marriage work. Dad was right—she was a courageous woman. She'd tried very hard to live a traditional life and to make us happy. I'd been so wrapped up in my own shocked feelings that I hadn't looked at the situation from any other point of view. I missed having Mom in my life. I wanted us to joke and laugh like we used to. And I wanted to share the good moments in my life with her—like meeting Brad.

Shortly before midnight, the nurse returned and said that Mom was breathing on her own and that we could see her even though she was still sedated. Samantha, Dad, and I followed the nurse back into Mom's room. Mom's face was still pale and her arms were still hooked up to IVs, but it was a relief not to hear the mechanical click of the ventilator and to see that Mom no longer had the plastic breathing tube.

"This is a Thanksgiving I'll never forget," Brad said as we got into his car to go home. It was almost one o'clock in the morning and snow was beginning to fall.

"I'm going to work at getting back my relationship with my mom," I said.

I was at Mom's side as she recovered from her operation and we grew closer day by day. I opened up more fully to Samantha, and our friendship also began to build. I learned valuable lessons from Brad and Dad about how personal shock and pain can keep you from seeing situations from everyone's perspective. Thanks to their wisdom, I found my way back to my mother.

THE END

NOTHING TO BE THANKFUL FOR
But I convinced him to keep living

"How can you even suggest having Thanksgiving dinner here?" my husband shouted. "There'll be no Thanksgiving in this house, Julia. I have nothing to be thankful for . . . nothing." Ethan stormed out of the house, slamming the door behind him.

Tears streamed down my cheeks. The man I'd married seven months before, the man who'd loved me as tenderly and as passionately as a man could love, just said he had nothing to be thankful for.

I'm not sure what I'd expected. We'd both gone through hell and back during the past six months. But now that November was here and Thanksgiving was just three weeks away, it seemed the perfect time to begin the healing we needed so much. I'd talked to both our parents the day before and they agreed it might help to be together this first holiday without Benjamin. We even decided to include Benjamin's mom. Kim was alone, her parents both gone, her only son buried six months ago.

"It might help us begin to heal," I'd said to Ethan's mom just last night.

There'd been a long pause and I could hear muffled cries. I could've kicked myself for making her cry again. There'd been too many tears.

"Liz, I'm sorry. Don't cry, please. We just need to somehow find peace."

I could hear her blow her nose, then my mother-in-law said, "I know you're right, Julia. But I don't know how Ethan will feel about this. He still blames himself. You know that."

I sighed. "Of course I do. That's why I thought if we were all together we might be able to make some sense of it. I feel guilty, too, Liz. If I hadn't married Ethan, his son—your grandson—might still be alive."

"Don't even think that," she said. "I loved Benjamin with all my heart, but he was a very troubled young man. And he was troubled long before you met Ethan. His mother's drinking affected the whole family. If anyone was to blame, it was Kim. What a shame it took her son's suicide to finally sober her up."

"Has she really stayed sober?" I asked, having heard that from friends of Ethan's, but never able to talk to him about it.

"Yes. Apparently she feels it's the only way to honor her son's life. To make something of her own."

"Benjamin would've been proud of her," I murmured.

"Yes. After all she put him and this family through, at least this would have pleased him. Too bad it couldn't have happened while he was still alive." I could hear the bitterness in my mother-in-law's voice.

"Liz, you've never talked to me about Kim's drinking before."

"I never liked talking about it," she said softly. "And I don't like divorce, either. I wasn't happy when Ethan initiated it, even though I knew the whole thing was a terrible burden on him. He felt if he broke off with her, she might get herself together for Benjamin's sake."

"But she never did."

Another pause. "No. Kim seemed to get even worse after the divorce. Ethan even asked Benjamin to come and live with him, but the boy felt he owed it to his mother to be there for her. I think he had hopes of getting her to quit drinking so his father would come back home."

Her words felt like a knife in my heart. Tears sprang to my eyes. The boy had wanted his mother and father back together again.

"But then he met me," I said, barely able to stop the tears.

"Julia, it's no one's fault that you two met and fell in love. Ethan hadn't had a loving woman in his life for years. He tried his best; he really tried to help Kim. When she started pulling him down with her, he had to leave. We all knew he couldn't go on any longer. Everyone gave him credit for waiting until Benjamin was seventeen and out of high school. Ethan's a good man."

"The best," I murmured.

"I'll talk to him about Thanksgiving, Julia. Maybe I can make him understand why you want to do this. Why we all need to come together."

I prayed that she could.

When I'd met Ethan at a joint luncheon for our two insurance agencies almost two years ago, I'd liked him immediately. He had such a warm smile and when he shook my hand after we were introduced, I'd felt very comfortable with him. During the luncheon I found myself talking to him as easily as if I'd known him all my life. We didn't see each other often, but when our jobs did put us together for a meeting or a class, we picked up where we'd left off the time before. We definitely enjoyed each other's company.

The first time Ethan called and invited me to meet him for lunch, I was surprised but quickly agreed. By the end of that lunch, I was already falling in love with him.

It was on our fourth date that Ethan told me about his ex-wife. He'd been divorced for almost a year. He didn't blame Kim for the divorce, simply told me he couldn't handle the drinking and hoped she'd be able to get sober once he was gone. He also told me about his son, who was almost eighteen, and how concerned he was that the boy's mother would ruin his life.

During the year and a half that I dated Ethan, I often saw Benjamin. He was a handsome young man, a bit sullen, but then eighteen-year-olds frequently were. We included him in our lives as often as we could. Baseball games, picnics at my place, ice skating in the winter, even a movie now and then.

Only when we started talking about getting married did Benjamin get angry. "I thought you were 'just friends,' Dad," he shouted. "That's what you always told me. You and Julia were just friends."

Ethan was very patient and I remained silent. "Friends sometimes fall in love, son. That's what happened with Julia and me. Please be happy for me. She's a very special lady and I want her in my life."

"If she's in, I'm out." With those words Benjamin walked away. I felt awful for Ethan but he reassured me. "He'll be back, you wait and see. Who could resist you? You're so lovable." Ethan pulled me in his arms and kissed me and I forgot about Benjamin for a little while.

Shortly after Benjamin's outburst, a year and a half after we met, Ethan and I were married in a simple ceremony with only our four parents witnessing our marriage. Benjamin told his father he would not come.

Ethan wanted him there so much. I went to see Benjamin, to try and make him understand how much I loved his father, how much we both wanted him at our wedding. But he wouldn't listen. He was angry. He'd wanted his parents to get back together even then, almost three years after their divorce.

Ethan told me not to worry about it. "He'll come around eventually," he said. "When he realizes how much we love each other and how happy you make me, he'll be happy for me, too."

But Benjamin never did come around. Just a month after we were married, a month filled with joyful days and nights with a husband I adored, Benjamin ended his life. He took a gun from his mother's closet and shot himself.

The horror of it almost killed Ethan, too. He blamed himself for not talking to his son enough, for not caring enough about his feelings. "We should've waited longer," he told me. "I should've let him get to know you better."

I'd held him while he cried. I stood beside him at the funeral home, Kim on the other side of the closed casket. It was the first time I'd ever met her. She was in bad shape and my heart ached for her, too, even though I knew how much she'd hurt Ethan and all the family. She'd lost her only son.

Photos of Benjamin with his parents were displayed in the funeral home. There was one of his high school graduation, another of him as a toddler with a parent on either side of him, holding his chubby little hands.

But it was the photo of a tiny baby with eyes just like his father's that almost made me lose my composure. I was trying to be strong because Ethan was so vulnerable at that point. Yet that photo made me realize that Kim had loved Ethan back then as much as I loved him now and, because of their love, a child had been born—a child with his father's eyes.

Oddly enough, as Ethan fell apart after the funeral, Kim seemed to grow stronger. From what my mother-in-law told me, it was her son's death that finally got Kim sober. She blamed herself for his suicide, but unlike Ethan, who grew more despondent day by day, Kim felt she owed it to her son to make something of her life.

I'd gone to see her that morning, a few hours before I approached Ethan about Thanksgiving. I wanted to be sure she'd feel comfortable accepting my invitation.

Her eyes had welled up with tears when I told her what I wanted to do—for Benjamin, for our families, for healing that was so needed for all of us.

"I can't believe you'd even want me there, Julia. And I'm sure Ethan won't. I've done so much harm to this family for so many years. I don't deserve to be forgiven." She started to cry then, softly but steadily. I felt awkward but reached out to her, putting my arm around her shoulder. "Everyone deserves forgiveness, Kim."

She nodded, then stood taller and got her tears under control. "How's Ethan doing?"

I shook my head. "Not good. We both feel guilty about Benjamin's death. He obviously didn't want us to get married. Ethan honestly believed he'd come to our wedding even though he'd said he wouldn't. When he never showed up it hurt Ethan a lot. And when Benjamin ended his life, Ethan was certain it was because of our marriage."

"So we all go on blaming ourselves," Kim said.

I nodded. "That's why I felt if we came together on this first holiday without Benjamin, we might be able to make some sense of it. Talk it all out and start to heal from all the pain."

"If Ethan agrees to this, I'll come," she said. "But don't feel bad if he doesn't, Julia. He loved our son very much. It's going to take a while for him to get through this, I'm sure."

As I left Kim's house, I realized she knew Ethan better than I did. Before she'd begun drinking, they'd had a lot of good years together. She'd known him more than twenty years. I hardly knew him at all.

But I loved him. And I had hopes of having many more than

twenty years with him. In order to go on, though, I knew we had to somehow make sense of Benjamin's death.

When Ethan came home later that day, he took me in his arms and apologized. "I'm sorry I stormed out of there, babe. I just couldn't believe what you were suggesting. Thanksgiving. The word makes me cringe. How could any of us be thankful for anything this year?"

I tried my hardest not to cry, but the tears came unbidden. "I'm thankful, Ethan, for our love. I thank God every day for meeting you. I'd given up on ever finding a man who was honest and kind and fun to be with, a man who loved me for the person I was, a man who didn't look at me as a sex object, but a partner for life. But I found that man and I love him and I thank God for you every day of my life."

Ethan caressed my face, his thumbs wiping away my tears. "I love you, too, Julia, but my heart aches so much I can't even show you anymore."

"That's why we need this time together, Ethan. Maybe if you and your parents, me and my parents, and Kim can get together and talk about Benjamin, we can make some sense out of what's happened."

"My mother told me that, too."

"You saw her today?"

He nodded, still caressing my face. "Kim won't come," he said.

"Yes, she will. She will if it's okay with you."

"You asked her already?"

"I wanted to know if she'd consider it, before I even mentioned it to you," I said, hoping my husband would understand.

He dropped his hands at his side, staring at me with those compassionate eyes. I waited and finally he said, "All right. Do it. But don't expect me to be the happy host."

"None of us expects to be happy this holiday, Ethan. But we can at least be together."

The last few days before the holiday I was busy shopping and cleaning. My mom and Ethan's mom both called and offered to bring something for the dinner. The day before Thanksgiving Kim called.

"Is Thanksgiving still on?" she asked.

"Yes it is. I don't think any of us can cancel Thanksgiving. It just comes whether we want it to or not."

There was a pause and when Kim spoke again I could almost hear the smile in her voice. "Right. Just wasn't sure it was on at your house with me in attendance."

"You were Benjamin's mother. Ethan's parents were your in-laws long before they were mine. I think it's very important that the people who loved Benjamin the most are together tomorrow."

"I appreciate that, Julia." Another long pause. I was ready to speak when she asked, "Can I bring a dessert or something?"

81

"Yes, anything would be appreciated. I'm doing the turkey, stuffing, and potatoes. Liz's bringing her green bean casserole and my mom's making a pumpkin pie. Whatever you'd like to contribute will be great."

"Okay. I'll see what I can come up with."

"If you don't feel like making anything, please don't worry about it," I added.

"No. I really want to. It's just been a while since I've cooked or baked. I usually open a can of soup or that canned spaghetti. Just haven't had much of an appetite."

"I understand. We haven't been eating regular meals, either. This will be good for all of us."

Thanksgiving morning dawned gray and gloomy. I'd hoped for sunshine at least, to raise our spirits. I tried to remember that above all those dark clouds, the sun was shining. We just couldn't see it.

I got up early to get the turkey in the oven. For once, Ethan was still asleep. He hadn't been sleeping well since his son's death, so I tiptoed out and shut the door.

I'd just finished stuffing the turkey and putting it in the oven when Ethan came into the kitchen.

"Good morning," I said. "Happy Thanksgiving."

He put his arms around me and kissed me. "Good morning. But it's not happy, you know."

I nodded. "I know."

We had coffee and toast, as we did most mornings. And soon the kitchen smelled like Thanksgiving. There's nothing like a roasting turkey to make you hungry. By the time I'd set the dining room table, peeled the potatoes, and cooked a pot of creamed corn—my mom's favorite—it felt a bit more like a holiday.

Ethan helped with the table, even basted the turkey once, but I had no doubt he was thinking of other holidays with his son.

I said a silent prayer that what I hoped to accomplish would come to pass. I had no idea how Ethan or the rest of the family would react to what I'd planned. But I believed in prayer and I knew God had led me to gather this family together.

An hour before dinner my parents arrived, followed shortly thereafter by Ethan's mom and dad. We hugged and there were tears in Liz's eyes as well as Ethan's.

My dad had just lifted the turkey out of the oven when the doorbell rang again. "I'll get it," I said.

"I'll mash the potatoes," my mom said.

"I'll make the gravy," Liz said.

I nodded, glad they understood that I needed a moment with Kim. It wasn't easy having my husband's first wife in our home.

Ethan followed me to the door.

Kim stood out on the porch, a large box in her arms. She was looking up at the sky with a smile on her face. "Look, Ethan," she said. "It just started snowing. Remember how much Benjamin loved snow?"

He nodded and the three of us stood there, looking up at huge, puffy flakes tumbling from the sky.

Then Ethan smiled.

I could've hugged Kim. It was the perfect thing for her to say.

"It's snowing," I called out. Soon everyone was there on the porch looking up at the sky filled with millions of snowflakes—as though none of us had ever seen snow before.

Then we were all busy, Dad carving the turkey, the two moms getting vegetables on the table, and Kim unpacking her box. "I brought a sweet potato pie, something I always made for Thanksgiving, and my homemade bread."

Ethan had just come into the kitchen. "Homemade bread? It's been a long time, Kim."

She nodded. "A very long time, Ethan."

"He loved that bread."

"I know," she said.

Silent moments kept punctuating our conversations. Then Kim started slicing the bread and everyone got busy carrying serving platters and bowls to the dining room.

When we were all at our places, I asked if it would be all right if I said grace. I got nods of approval, and then asked everyone to join hands.

"Heavenly Father," I began. "On this Thanksgiving day, I ask You to look down on us as we gratefully thank You for all the blessings You have given us. We especially want to thank You for the life of a young man we all loved. There is sorrow at his leaving us, but we know he is safe in Your care. Thank You, too, for letting us all come together to celebrate Benjamin's life and to heal from his death."

Heads were bowed and Ethan's hand gripped mine. I paused, and then asked if each person gathered at the table could thank God for one thing they remembered about Benjamin.

This was the first thing I'd planned and for a long, agonizing moment of silence, I thought it was going to end before it began. Then my dad, bless his heart, spoke up.

"I'd like to thank God for bringing Ethan into our lives or we'd have never gotten to know Benjamin. I thank God for that boy's hearty handshake. I like a young man who knows how to shake hands."

With barely a pause, Liz spoke up. "I'm thankful for the grandson I loved with all my heart. I thank God for nineteen years with him. I thank God for his beautiful smile."

Next, Ethan's dad thanked God for the times he and his grandson went fishing together. "That boy knew how to bait a hook."

My mom thanked God for Benjamin's smile. "He had a smile that reached his eyes," she said. "That's a sincere smile."

Kim went next, as tears flowed down her cheeks, dripping onto the white linen tablecloth. "I thank God for my baby boy and for the young man he grew into. He was the joy of my life and I thank God he loved me despite my faults."

Ethan still hadn't made a move to speak, so I spoke next. "I am thankful for baseball games with Benjamin, for picnics, and movies. I'm thankful that he had such a bright mind and could discuss just about any subject in the world. But most of all, I thank God for those clear eyes, eyes so like his father's."

Liz and my mom were sniffling and tears continued to slip down Kim's cheeks.

Only Ethan was left. Everyone waited expectantly. Ethan said nothing.

I glanced up at him and squeezed his hand. "I'm sorry," he said. "My son is dead and I'm not thankful for that."

"You had nineteen years with your son," I said. "How dare you not be thankful for those years. By not saying one thing that you can be thankful for, you insult his mother, who gave birth to that beautiful baby. You make your parents' hearts ache even more because you can't find one thing in those nineteen years of his life to be thankful for.

"None of us has forgotten Benjamin's death, Ethan. We're simply trying to remember his life today. Your son lived for nineteen years. He made you laugh, and he made you proud. He looked up at you when he was a little boy and smiled that brilliant smile. He held your hand and he still holds your heart. If you can't be thankful for any of that, then be thankful that it's snowing because he loved snow, and be thankful that Kim baked his favorite homemade bread."

Everyone was looking at me, including my husband. "Would you rather he'd never been born, Ethan?"

Tears finally spilled from my husband's eyes. "Of course not."

"Then thank God for giving him to you."

Ethan closed his eyes and murmured, "I'm thankful for the little boy I had, for the man he became. I thank God for all the time I had with my son."

"Amen," I added.

We all hugged and wiped our tears away, relieved that Ethan had finally been able to say something about Benjamin.

Then we ate and we complimented everyone on the food they made and my mom and mother-in-law told me I'd done exceptionally well for roasting my first turkey.

Through all the dinner conversation, Kim was very quiet. I tried drawing her out, to get her to participate, but got mostly nods or "uh-huhs."

After dinner I served coffee and pie and everyone again raved about Kim's sweet potato pie, as they had about her bread.

"It was Benjamin's favorite pie for Thanksgiving," she said. "At least it was the last time I made it. Probably my last sober holiday before today."

Suddenly Kim was talking and she didn't stop there.

"I owe everyone here an apology," she continued. "I caused Ethan and my in-laws a tremendous amount of grief. Through the years, as I became addicted to alcohol, I did some things I'm not proud of. Some things I've done disgust me." She paused and everyone in the room sat with forks in hand or mid-air as they stopped eating.

"Julia, I haven't known you very long," she continued, "but you and your folks have been around long enough to know I was a terrible drunk. I almost cost Ethan his job a couple of times and Benjamin couldn't even bring his friends home because his mother was constantly 'sick' . . . that's what he said to hide my alcoholism.

"I've done some awful things during these past ten years or so, but the worst thing, by far, was not telling you, Ethan and Julia, that Benjamin had decided to go to your wedding."

Her words went straight to my soul. I was stunned. I could see Ethan was, too. He sat there, staring at her as she continued. "The night before your wedding day, he told me he loved his dad and if Julia made his father happy, then he'd have to accept that."

Ethan stood and went over to Kim's chair.

"What happened then, Kim?" he asked.

She looked up at him and said, "Benjamin ironed a shirt and found a tie to go with his blue jacket. He had everything laid out for the morning. When he went to bed, he was whistling the Wedding March."

My heart skipped a beat, my chest ached, as I imagined Benjamin whistling the Wedding March, planning to come to our wedding.

"I couldn't sleep," Kim went on. "All I could think about was the fact that I could lose my son to the two of you. He wasn't angry with you anymore. He finally realized there was no hope for you and me, Ethan.

"I felt like I was drowning. I drank a lot that night. I don't clearly remember the next day. Vague memories are still clouded in my mind. The day after your wedding, Benjamin told me he'd found me on the kitchen floor the morning of your wedding. At first he thought I was dead, then I moaned and he knew I was just drunk. He made coffee and poured it into me. He was still going to try and make it to your wedding." Kim paused, and no one moved or spoke.

"He told me . . . he said . . . I begged him not to go. I don't know what I said. I'm sure I heaped on the guilt—I was good at that, wasn't I, Ethan?" Kim looked up at him, her cheeks streaked with tears.

"He wanted to come to your wedding but I made him feel like he'd be betraying me if he did. Now do you understand? Do you all understand? None of you ever has to feel guilty again. I tore that boy in half. I pulled at him until he didn't know which way to turn. I might as well have taken the gun and killed him myself."

I sat in stunned disbelief. Benjamin had been planning to come to our wedding.

I felt a great burden of guilt lifted from my shoulders. I turned to Ethan, who was crying harder than he'd cried since the day Benjamin died. "It's all right," I crooned as I held him in my arms. "He was coming. He did care."

Ethan's mom and dad came over and hugged their son. My parents held me in a group hug.

When we finally stopped hugging and talking, we turned to find Kim heading for the front door. "Kim, don't go," I called out to her.

"You don't need me here anymore, Julia. You all know the truth now. Benjamin loved his dad and he was coming around to loving you, too. I kept him from a very important moment in his father's life. I'm responsible for his death. I don't deserve your concern or your forgiveness."

"I told you a few weeks back that everyone deserves forgiveness," I said. "If Benjamin were here, you know he'd forgive you."

She nodded and tears continued to stream from her eyes.

"I just thank you for telling us," I said. "This is the healing I'd prayed for and God's answered my prayers. He's used you, Kim, to begin the healing."

The rest of the evening we spent looking at all the old photo albums I'd resurrected from the basement. It was the second thing I'd planned for this holiday—reliving the past, revisiting happy times.

We paid tribute to Benjamin that night and finally found some peace in the knowledge that he'd wanted to be with us on our wedding day.

After everyone left, I sat next to my husband on the sofa. "Are you still angry about us having Thanksgiving here today?"

He shook his head. "First of all, I could never be angry at you," he said. "And how could anyone be angry after learning that my son wanted to give his blessing on our marriage? That's a heavy load that's been lifted off my shoulders, babe."

I snuggled against him, still holding a photo of the baby Benjamin had been.

"How would you like to start all over?" I asked.

He seemed a bit puzzled. "Start what all over?"

"With another one of these," I said, pointing to the photo of Benjamin as a baby.

"You mean? We're . . ."

"Yes," I murmured. "We're going to have a baby . . . in about five months."

"You're four months pregnant?" Ethan asked.

I nodded. "I found out over a month ago."

"Why didn't you tell me sooner?" he asked.

I ran my hand along his cheek, trying to wipe away the months of worry etched into his face. "I couldn't begin to plan for a new life until we were all at peace about Benjamin. I prayed it would go well today. I got much more than I prayed for."

"And I got my son back," he said. "And another one on the way," he added, gently caressing my abdomen with his hand.

"Or daughter," I said.

THE END

MORE THAN A NEIGHBOR
The Best Thanksgivings Are Unplanned.

Billows of smoke streamed from the oven. I grabbed a dishtowel and started fanning as my six-year-old daughter joined me in the kitchen.

"Mama, what's burning?" Haylie asked.

I turned off the oven and flapped the dishtowel harder. Smoke was still pouring out of the appliance that I was quickly growing to hate. I hurried to open a window as I heard the smoke detector scream.

I could hear Nick, my four-year-old, cry in the living room.

"Haylie, it's going to be all right. I think I just got the turkey a little over-cooked.

Haylie gave me a look that told me she knew burnt when she smelled it.

"Could you please go see what's wrong with your brother?"

"I think Nick's hungry. When will dinner be ready?" she asked.

I glanced around my kitchen. It looked like a fraternity house after a food fight.

"Honey, I don't know."

She gave me an eye roll. "This is Thanksgiving, Mommy."

"Yes, honey, I'm aware of the date. It's just that I'm not real good at this cooking thing."

More eye-rolling as she left the kitchen. I wasn't looking forward to those teen years.

The thought of having to feed my children peanut butter and jelly sandwiches for Thanksgiving dinner filled me with such despair that I wanted to sit down at my cluttered kitchen table and cry.

Our lives had really changed in just one year. Last Thanksgiving, my children and I, along with my then-husband, had been a happy family. At least that's what I'd thought. Every year we went to my in-laws' house for Thanksgiving. Like many married women, I had a cool relationship with my mother-in-law, mostly because she worshipped my husband. He was her only child and could do no wrong in her eyes. She loved her grandchildren but just tolerated me.

Thanksgiving was a huge deal to her. She cooked for days and her house was spotless. The dinner was wonderful, but I always felt that her protests against my bringing anything and against needing any help in the kitchen was more about her dislike for me than anything else.

I admit that I'm a lousy cook. My mother had been the queen of takeout food. I didn't have a good teacher. My grandmother had left me some of her recipes, but I'd never been given much instruction. Now I wished that I had tried harder to learn how to cook. I hadn't made the time, and now I was paying the price.

Looking back on our life, I should have seen the signs. My husband started acting odd, staying out late and going off on the weekends. My job kept me busy, and the children filled up the rest of the time.

I shouldn't have been shocked when John told me that he had met someone else and wanted a divorce. Of course, my mother-in-law blamed me. She was furious with me, demanding to know what I had done to drive her son into the arms of another woman.

I wanted to tell her that I'd put up with her cheating son for months and that he was the one wanting out of the marriage, but I knew that it would be a waste of breath.

When the company that I worked for as a secretary relocated their offices six months later, I jumped at the chance to move away. Although they did offer a relocation package, it was still a challenge to make ends meet. My kids and I were now in an apartment five hundred miles away. We were also alone with no family nearby. I was a single mother with no support system. Funny though, I was starting to feel happier than I had been when I was married and foolishly thought that everything was fine.

Even with the help from my company, it hadn't been easy relocating. Moving is a huge expense. Finding an apartment that I could afford and getting the utilities turned on had emptied my bank account. Everyone wanted hookup fees and deposits.

I looked at the mess that was my kitchen and cursed myself for never learning to cook. It would have made my life easier and less expensive. I wondered if any of the fast-food places were open on Thanksgiving Day.

I got up from the kitchen table, determined to salvage whatever I could of the holiday. I opened the apartment door to start airing out the smoke and saw my neighbor peeking out from behind his door.

"I'm sorry," I said to the handsome man across the hall. "I've had a little problem with the turkey."

"Oh, I was wondering where all the smoke was coming from," he said as he looked into my apartment.

I was surprised that he even spoke to me. The kids and I had seen him in the building, but he never really seemed friendly, so I never introduced us. I'd decided to keep a low profile. I knew that my kids could be noisy, and I didn't want to draw attention to us. I also knew that as a single mother, I didn't want to look like an easy target. My neighbor was equally quiet and had kept to himself. I didn't know his name. I wasn't even sure if he lived alone or not, but I didn't think that I had seen anyone with him on the few times that we'd met going in or out.

Haylie joined me at the door.

"Mom, I'm hungry. When is Thanksgiving dinner going to be ready?"

I smiled at the neighbor and turned to my daughter.

"Honey, I've had a little problem with the turkey. The rest of the dinner will be ready soon." This was very much wishful thinking on my part.

"Mommy, the smoke is making my eyes water."

She was right. It wasn't nice in my apartment now. But where could I take them on Thanksgiving Day?

I could tell that my neighbor wasn't exactly thrilled with the idea, but he said, "Uh, you're welcome to stay at my apartment until the smoke clears."

I turned to him, trying to think of a reason to refuse his invitation, but one look into my daughter's eyes told me that I had no choice.

"I hate to impose on you on the holiday," I said.

"It's no problem, really," he said.

Haylie perked up. "Please, Mommy." She coughed twice for dramatic effect.

"Are you sure we wouldn't be in your way?"

"I'm sure."

I retrieved my youngest child from the living room where he was engrossed in the Thanksgiving Day parade. I also grabbed some of the food that I had been attempting to prepare.

"My name is Amy Huston, and these are my children, Haylie and Nick." My brood and I shuffled across the hall.

"Nice to meet you. I'm Paul Johnston. Let me help you with that dish."

"I was attempting to fix Thanksgiving dinner, but as you've probably been able to tell already, I'm not a very good cook."

He just nodded and smiled.

His apartment was neat and clean. I immediately worried that my kids would mess it up or spill something on his nice carpet or sofa.

"Mom, look at that huge TV," Haylie said as I settled the kids in Paul's living room.

The TV was an enormous flat screen.

"I haven't had it long. I don't watch a lot of television, but I do like to catch some sports from time to time," Paul said.

He picked up a remote, and the television sprang to life.

"Wow, this is cool," Haylie said as she settled on the floor.

Paul turned on the Thanksgiving parade, and both kids were mesmerized.

"I really want to thank you for this. The kids have been looking forward to Thanksgiving so much. I'm so mad at myself for ruining our turkey."

"It's no problem," Paul said, although I sensed that he wasn't entirely happy with our intrusion.

"We won't stay long. I'm sure you have your own plans for the day." I hadn't smelled any turkey cooking, so I didn't think that he was preparing dinner. He could be having company. The apartment was neat and tidy, although it didn't quite look like it was going to be the place for a family gathering.

"Come on in the kitchen. Let's put your food down."

Paul led me into his kitchen, which was also neat and clean and looked very lived-in. He had a beautiful butcher-block knife set and an array of pots hanging from hooks in the ceiling.

"I don't want to keep you from your plans today."

"Really, it's okay. I was just going to watch football."

I guess not everyone has family or friends to spend the holiday with.

"Would you like a soft drink, or maybe a beer?" he asked.

"Something cold would be good. Whatever you have is fine."

Paul handed me a cold can of soda and I popped it open and took a sip. The cold liquid felt wonderful in my throat after all the smoke I'd been inhaling.

"This is really good. Cooking that dinner was making me crazy," I said.

He smiled and motioned for me to take a seat on one of the stools at his counter.

So many questions flooded my mind. Is Paul married? Does he live here alone? Why doesn't he have any real plans for the holiday? Of course I couldn't ask.

I felt terrible about the ruined dinner. I wondered what I was going to do to feed the kids. They were expecting a big feast. The parade would only keep them occupied for so long, and then they would be fussing to be fed.

"Paul, my kids are getting hungry. Do you mind if I fix them a sandwich or something?"

Paul looked at me. "Oh, sure. Your whole dinner isn't ruined, is it?"

I thought for a moment. Could something actually be salvaged?

"I do have some canned green beans that I was going to try to make into a casserole, and I have potatoes to cook and mash."

"Good, let me help. I'm not too bad of a cook."

He was probably thinking that nobody could be as bad a cook as me, but he was kind enough not to say it.

91

Paul started pulling pots off the hooks and opening drawers.

"Thanksgiving dinner can be a challenge, even for experienced cooks. It's a lot of work, and timing is very important."

He opened his pantry doors and rummaged around.

"I thought that I had a couple of boxes of stuffing," he said as he placed the mixes on the counter.

He then started rummaging around in his refrigerator.

"Why don't you get your potatoes? I think that we can throw together a modest Thanksgiving dinner, but what we don't have is a turkey."

Guilt flooded back.

He pulled open his freezer and produced a stack of frozen turkey dinners.

"I was actually going to eat one of these later. They aren't too bad, and I think with the rest of the stuff we can make a passable dinner.

I gave him a questioning look.

"Yes, this will work," he said.

I ran over to the apartment. The smoke had thinned out, but it still smelled bad. The turkey was a disaster. It had been incinerated beyond repair. Even Rachael Ray wouldn't have been able to save it. I grabbed the bag of potatoes, along with a pumpkin pie and a container of whipped cream. A couple cans of refrigerated crescent roll dough and a packet of gravy mix went into a plastic bag. Back at Paul's apartment, we quickly got to work. I started peeling the potatoes while Paul dumped the contents of the stuffing mixes into a large pan. Once the potatoes were finished, he set them in a large pot of water and turned on the heat.

"I wish I learned how to cook," I said.

"It isn't really too hard. My parents believed that boys should be taught to cook. My dad was a pretty good cook, but my mother was the best."

He stopped for a moment, probably thinking back to past Thanksgivings.

"You're lucky. My mother barely knew how to boil water."

"Well, then don't be too hard on yourself. Everyone needs a teacher."

"I guess. It's tough to find the time to learn with my job and the kids."

"What kind of work do you do?"

"I'm a secretary for Gibson Manufacturing. They relocated me from Springfield when they closed the plant there. I was lucky to have a job."

"I know what you mean. I'm a carpenter, and it's tough staying in work through the year. It really slows down during the holidays." He stopped again, absorbed in thought.

I felt encouraged to tell him more. I hadn't had any really close friends, and my casual friends had been left back in Springfield.

"It hasn't been easy being a single mother. I just got divorced a year and a half ago." I wasn't sure why I was confiding in him, but it felt good to talk.

"I'm sorry to hear that," he said.

He didn't offer any information about his own marital status, so I had to assume that he had never been married.

As the potatoes and stuffing cooked, he readied the oven for the green bean casserole. Once the potatoes were done, Paul whipped them with his mixer and added milk and butter. They looked delicious. The kids were going to love them and hopefully wouldn't miss having a big turkey.

As the rolls browned in the oven, Paul whisked some milk into the powdered packets of gravy.

My job was to microwave the frozen turkey dinners. I guess he figured that I'd be safe with the microwave. Once they were heated, he carefully placed the slices of turkey on a platter.

"Well, that isn't the perfect turkey, but I think it will taste pretty good," he said.

"It looks wonderful. Thank you so much. I'm sure this wasn't what you had planned for your holiday."

He got that far-off look on his face again, and I wondered if I would ever find out what he was thinking of.

I quickly set the table with beautiful dishes that Paul had in his cupboard.

Haylie came into the kitchen. "Mommy, I smell something good," she said with a surprised voice.

"Dinner is just about ready. Go get your brother and help him wash his hands."

Everything was out of the oven. Minutes later, the food was on the table.

"Thank you so much, Mr. Johnston," I said.

"Please, call me Paul. I was glad to help."

"Yeah, thanks," said Haylie as she started digging into her food

I helped Nick with a piece of turkey, and he pushed a large spoonful of mashed potatoes into his mouth.

I took a tentative bite of mashed potatoes, and my taste buds rejoiced. The buttery mound melted in my mouth.

I then tried a bite of the microwaved frozen turkey. It was better than I had expected.

I had to admit that the meal was delicious. The kids ate hungrily. Paul even seemed to enjoy himself.

This was one of the nicest Thanksgiving dinners I'd ever had, and I didn't even have to put up with my opinionated mother-in-law. Her cooking had been to die for, but it came with a big price.

After dinner, the kids settled in front of the television again to watch the football game.

I insisted that Paul sit and relax while I cleaned up in the kitchen. Despite my terrible cooking skills, this dinner hadn't turned out too bad. I filled the sink with hot soapy water and let a couple of the pots soak. I loaded the dishwasher and started it. All but a slice or two of the turkey had been eaten. The leftover mashed potatoes went into a plastic container.

"You really don't have to clean up."

I was startled to see Paul in the kitchen doorway.

"Sure I do. You were so nice to open your home to us on a holiday."

"I have to admit, it was fun. I'd just planned on eating a frozen dinner and watch football all day."

"I hope that we didn't interrupt your plans."

He had that far away look again, and I hoped that he hadn't canceled plans to be here for us.

"No, no plans other than the game."

The game that he wasn't watching. I thought of the kids. Maybe they were bothering him.

I gave him a look of concern. "Are the kids okay? They aren't being a bother, are they?"

"Oh, no, the kids are great. I just wanted to see if you needed any help."

"No, I think I have everything cleaned up. Are you ready for some pie?" I asked. "I didn't make it, so it should be good." I was really glad that I'd decided not to try and bake a pumpkin pie.

"Maybe in a few minutes," he said.

Now I was worried. Maybe he did think it was time for us to leave.

"I can check my apartment. The smoke has probably cleared enough for us to go home."

"No. Stay. I want to tell you something."

Geez, what could that be? I wondered.

We both sat on the stools at his kitchen counter.

"I'm sorry that I haven't been very friendly and welcoming to you and your children."

I was confused. "What do you mean? You've been so nice today."

He nodded. "I mean, I wasn't very friendly when you first moved in."

"That's okay," I said.

"No, it isn't. I need to explain."

He took a big breath and continued. "I was married. My wife died a few years ago."

"I'm so sorry," I said.

94

He continued. "Since then, I've really had no desire to celebrate anything—including holidays. Seeing happy families made me miss my wife and the children we never had even more. I've locked myself away in this apartment. I believed that I was honoring her memory by obsessing about her—just moping around, really. Over the fact that she's no longer here with me."

My heart was aching for this nice man.

"I realize now, being with you and your wonderful children, that I've been missing my life. Angie wouldn't have wanted me to pine away for her forever."

I tried to understand what it must have been like for him to lose someone that he loved. I thought that, with my divorce, I could relate. But I very quickly realized that having a loved one leave you intentionally for someone else couldn't ever be compared to having your soul mate taken away unexpectedly, without either party's agreement, and never to return. The times that he saw us in the halls or outside must have been torturous.

"You don't have to apologize for anything. This has been one of the best Thanksgivings that I've ever had."

"I think it has been for me too."

We sat there for a few moments, deep in our own thoughts.

"I've decided that things are going to change—right now. I'm done mourning and hiding myself away from life."

I smiled and nodded, not sure what to say.

He smiled back and said, "Would you and the kids like to go to the circus next month? I saw an ad in the newspaper and I haven't gone in years."

"The kids would love that," I said.

"I think I'm ready for that pie now," he said.

"Coming right up.

THE END

SECOND HELPINGS
Love Is Served on Holidays.

"Only six pies this year? You're slipping, Amanda." Grandpa Sam's eyes twinkled as he teased me. His eyes greedily scanned the pecan, pumpkin, and lemon pies I'd brought. Two of each. They took three days to make, on top of all the other orders I had.

"I suppose that means you won't be tasting them, then," I teased.

I love Thanksgiving at Grandma and Grandpa's even more than Christmas. Most of the family hasn't seen each other all year and it's a time to catch up and eat some seriously good food. No one misses Thanksgiving.

I went into the big family room where the men were gathered around the game, of course. I passed out kisses, compliments, and congratulations when I was spotted a new baby bump or engagement ring.

Then I froze when I saw my cousin, Violet, in the corner. She was holding hands with someone who looked suspiciously like my high school boyfriend; the one who'd dumped me before prom, leaving me to wonder if I'd ever trust anyone with my heart again. I hadn't so far.

I wanted to bolt from the room, but she'd spotted me. She popped up from the couch and waved me over. I trudged over and she gave me a kiss on the cheek.

"Amanda! You look great. I want you to meet my boyfriend, Pete."

Pete stood up, his eyes wide. "Amanda Shepherd?"

I shrugged. "Yep. It's me. Guess you didn't know Violet is my cousin. Different last name and all."

He stumbled and bumbled his words. "No, I didn't."

Oh, he looked good. No surprise, since he looked good back in high school.

"How are you, Pete? It's been, like, seven years?"

Violet watched us, her mouth hanging open. "You two know each other?"

I jerked my thumb in his direction. "We dated senior year. He dumped me right before prom."

"Amanda, you make it sound so. . . ."

"Bad?"

He sank back on the couch. "It was bad. I'm sorry."

I waved a hand. "No worries. I'm over it. Just don't agree to go to any formals with him, Violet." I winked and walked away, looking and acting far more confident than I felt. Oh, this is going to be a long night trying to dodge the two of them.

I wandered to the kitchen, where I was quickly assigned the task of keeping an eye on the gravy. Lots of fun. I was stirring the thick, brown concoction and sampling the appetizers when Pete wandered into the kitchen with an empty glass.

"So, what are you up to these days?" he asked.

Looking for a decent man, which you're not. Which isn't true. Pete was a great guy in high school—funny, sweet, and all the things a girl could want. Except for the dumping me part. I looked up from my stirring.

"I just opened a little bakery in town. Rise and Shine." I blushed a little at the goofy name, but business had been good my first few months. My grandpa loaned me the money, convinced my homemade goodies would be a hit.

"A bakery? That's great," Pete said. "I'm working at an insurance agency in the city."

I grabbed a fresh spoon to sample the gravy. "Almost done," I said. "You're lucky to score an invitation to one of our Thanksgiving dinners. They're legendary. How did you meet Violet, anyway?"

"A bar. Typical."

"She's a great girl. Don't make me come and hurt you if you screw this up." I threatened him with my spoon.

He held up two hands in defense. "A baker with a bite. I've been warned. Well, nice seeing you, Amanda."

"You, too," I said, in a voice entirely more chipper than my heart was feeling.

I'd fallen hard for Pete in school. We flirted relentlessly during our junior year and he finally asked me out right after Homecoming our senior year. I guess we hadn't been serious enough to invite him to Thanksgiving that year, but we were an item for the next few months.

So, of course, I was busy getting ready for prom and all the trappings that went with it. Got the dress, booked the limo, and he broke up with me a week before.

"I can't go out with you anymore," he'd told me. No other explanation than that.

I went to prom anyway with some other single friends. I had a lousy time, spending each moment remembering that Pete was supposed to be there with me.

Pete and Violet were seated right across from me at the dinner table. Every time I looked up from my turkey, Violet was staring at Pete adoringly. I took thirds of Grandma's great stuffing, as if that could stuff back my bad feelings.

When the conversation lulled while everybody was busy scarfing down the feast, Violet piped up.

"How's this for a coincidence? Amanda and Pete used to date in high school."

All heads at the table snapped in my direction.

I gulped down my mouthful of yams. "And we all know that was a long time ago."

"Well, the Shepherd girls have always had great taste in men," Grandma said, squeezing Grandpa's hand.

"You seeing anyone now, Amanda?" Uncle Donnie asked.

I never did like Uncle Donnie, I thought to myself. "Nope. It's just my pies and goodies keeping me warm these days. Which reminds me, I should go slice them up. Looks like you guys will be ready for dessert soon."

Laughter skittered across the table as I dashed off to the kitchen. This was bothering me far more than it should. Maybe I was going through a quarter-life crisis like I'd read about, where you sort of evaluate where you are in life at twenty-five and decide it's not where you want to be.

I was a little more eager with the knife while carving up the pies. I got lots of compliments on my baking, as usual, and Pete even asked for seconds of my lemon pie.

An hour later, he and Violet were cuddled up on the couch and I decided to call it a night.

"Leaving so soon?" Grandpa Sam asked as I packed up my stuff.

"It's been a long day. I've got work to do tomorrow. I'm hoping for some hungry black Friday shoppers."

"And it's got nothing to do with your ex-boyfriend showing up with Violet?"

"Not at all," I said too quickly.

He kissed my head. "Well, then get to bed and sell some goodies tomorrow."

I slipped out the door without saying my usual good-byes to everyone. I just wanted to be by my miserable, lonely self.

Sure enough, business was booming Friday. I was too busy to think about Pete, but my girlfriends got an earful when we went out Saturday night.

"Who thinks Amanda's cousin should dump the guy now that she knows he was Amanda's true love?" Lisa asked for a show of drinks in agreement.

All four of my friends raised their beers.

"You guys can't be serious. It was six years ago in high school, for crying out loud. And he dumped me. He's a jerk. Let her have him." I picked at the label on my beer. "He looked amazing, hotter than I remembered and everything, but I'd be stupid to ever go out with him again. Right?"

My friends sat quietly, staring at me.

"What?"

"Methinks the lady doth protest too much," Cathy said.

"What, you think I still like him?"

Silence.

I downed the rest of my beer. "Well, even if I did, it's not like I'd ever steal him from Violet."

"Right," Lisa said. "Just keep reminding yourself of what a creep he was, dumping you before prom for no good reason."

"I surely will," I said, glad I had that shred of hatred to cling to.

I was hoping for a quiet Monday morning after the big holiday rush. I was going to bake and freeze some pies and get prepped for the next big stream of customers I expected as the holiday parties got into full swing. My first customer came in at eleven. I looked up and dropped the egg I was holding.

"Pete?"

He stood in front of my display case and crossed his arms. "Hey, Amanda. Cute place."

Hey, Pete, cute everything, I thought. "Got you hooked on my lemon pie, did I?"

He laughed. "It was good. I'll definitely be leaving with one of those." He sighed. "But I wanted to talk to you about how things ended between us."

I wrinkled my nose. "Why? It was so long ago."

"Because I was horrible to you." He looked at his shoes. "But I had a very good reason."

"A very good reason for dumping me right before prom." I crossed my arms and thought, This is gonna be good. Or bad.

He nodded his head and let out a breath. "I broke up with you before prom because I didn't have the money to take you."

"What?"

"I'd been trying to save up, but I didn't make enough at that busboy job. Then my dad lost his job a month before and he couldn't give me the money. I'm sorry. I was too embarrassed to tell you. It was easier to break up than admit I couldn't afford it."

I fiddled with the mound of dough in front of me. My throat felt thick. All those hours spent crying. All those moments I doubted myself, and my self-worth, were for nothing.

"So, you didn't want to break up with me?"

He laughed one of those sad laughs that don't sound funny at all. "No. I loved you, Amanda."

My chest hurt and I fought back the tears. "And now you love my cousin."

He opened his mouth, and then closed it. "I don't think we're at that point yet. It's only been two months."

My timer went off in the kitchen. "I've got to get that."

"Oh, sure. I want one of your lemon pies before I go, and your card. Our company's having an in-house holiday party in two weeks and your desserts would be a hit."

I forced a smile. "Thanks, that would be great." I handed him a card and wrapped up a pie for him. "On the house," I said, handing it to him.

He shook his head. "No, I'm paying for your talent. Don't worry; I've got the money now, Amanda. I'm doing very well for myself."

He left the money on the counter and I dashed back to the kitchen. I took the pies out of the oven and let myself cry.

It was very hard to push Pete out of my mind after finding out that he wasn't a schmuck. Lisa advised me to go for it anyway. I hate to admit that maybe I would if Violet wasn't my cousin. But she is, and I couldn't betray her like that. Luckily business was brisk and I could easily lose myself in mounds of flour and butter.

Until Pete called a week later to order twelve pies and five-dozen cookies for his company's party.

"I'll pick them up that morning," he said.

I couldn't sleep the night before he came in. It was like I was back in high school, hoping to cross his path in the halls between classes. When he walked in the next morning at ten, my stomach flip-flopped and I had to remind myself to be cool. He's dating my cousin and it's been years since we've been together. He's just a nice guy who wanted to clear his conscience.

"Thanks so much for this order, Pete."

"Thanks for taking it. I'm going to be a total hero back at the office." He grinned at me, and I remembered how nicely those lips of his had once kissed mine.

"So, are you coming to the Shepherd's Christmas Bash? I can promise you there'll just as many loud, obnoxious people, and just as much food. Plus a pie or two or six."

"Yeah, Violet mentioned it."

"How's that working out between you two?" Subtle.

He sighed. "We're both pretty busy these days. She's been a little frustrated with my work schedule."

I hate to admit I was very interested in this new development. I swallowed hard. "Yeah, sometimes I'm grateful I'm single. It would be tough to handle a relationship and a new business."

He raised an eyebrow. "I guess that's when you know you're with the right person. It seems easy. It just happens no matter what your schedule's like. You want to be with that person so badly that nothing gets in the way."

I nodded, remembering how it was like that in high school. "You're right. Now if only that right person would come along."

We stared at each other for a long moment and I turned to get his pies.

"We had that," he said quietly.

"Excuse me?"

"We had that in high school, didn't we?"

I set down the stack of pies and smiled. "We did. But we were teenagers. We didn't have all the pressures and responsibilities we do now."

He shrugged. "I guess you're right. But I was always wondered."

I totaled up his order and handed him his bill. I didn't want to be the person that broke him and Violet up, no matter how much I was still attracted to him.

"Thanks again, Pete. I'll see you at the Christmas party."

He nodded and walked out the door. My heart was a sad little lump in my chest. Can't have it all, baby, I told myself.

I went shopping for a new outfit for the Christmas season. I had a few parties to go to, not just the Shepherd bash, and so it wasn't like I was only buying it to look good in front of Pete. But, yeah, that was a big part of it. No harm in giving him a good look at what he lost, right?

But when I showed up at the party in my fur-trimmed red sweater on Christmas Eve, Violet was alone.

"Where's Pete?" I asked.

She sighed. "He broke up with me a week ago. Seems to be a thing with him, huh? Breaking up with women before big events." She shook her head and laughed. "He probably just didn't want to buy me a present."

"Oh, I don't think it was that. He stopped in my shop and said he was doing pretty well money-wise."

She sat up a little straighter. "He stopped by your shop?"

"Yeah, he ordered some pies for his company's Christmas party. That was all," I said quickly.

"Did he say anything about me?"

"No," I lied. I was not getting caught up in their drama.

"Jerk," she said, slumping back on the couch. "What kind of guy breaks up with a girl before prom? Or Christmas, for that matter. I should have dumped him when you told me that story."

"Well, you'll bounce back, Violet. A whole sea of fish out there, right?"

"Right."

But there was one fish I had my mind on. What's the proper grace period for a situation like this?

The New Year rolled in with fancy cake orders and lots of snow, but no Pete. I thought maybe now that he and Violet were through; he might stop back in the shop. Lisa and the girls concluded he was observing some sort of grace period, too, and predicted we'd be back together in a month.

I was starting to doubt their theory, but then on Valentine's Day a big bouquet of pink roses was delivered to me. I read the card. Interested in second chances? Pete.

Well, yeah, I thought, I am. But how do I reach you? I didn't have long to worry about that. He came in later that day and asked me to have dinner with him on Saturday night.

"Yes. Absolutely," I told him with a big smile.

I wore my fur-trimmed sweater again since I really did pick it out for him. He picked me up and I asked him where we were going.

He grinned. "You'll see."

We chatted and recalled good times as we drove across town. He pulled in front of The Crystal Ballroom and looked at me.

"Wow. I haven't been there in a while."

"Like since prom, maybe?"

"Yeah, this is where we had prom. One of the most miserable nights of my life, I might add." I playfully whacked his arm and he grabbed my hand and squeezed it.

"I'm sorry. I really am. I ruined what should have been one of your fondest high school memories. I know dinner tonight won't make up for it, but I was serious about second chances. I've never forgotten you, Amanda. Can we try again?"

I nodded, the words unable to work their way out of my mouth.

He hopped out of the car and opened my door. We had a wonderful dinner and ended up back at my place, sort of picking up where things left off.

And he was right. We did find time for each other. If I had orders to fill keeping me late at work, he helped, or kept me company talking to me, telling funny jokes. If he had reports due, I brought him dinner at the office. By the time Easter rolled around, we were a couple. One of those obnoxious couples everyone wants to hate.

"I don't feel comfortable bringing you to Easter brunch," I told Pete. "I'm not ready to tell Violet yet. I think she'd assume you broke up with her for me."

"I did," he said.

"You did?"

He nodded and kissed my head. "Couldn't stop thinking about you once I saw you at Thanksgiving dinner. I'd always wanted to explain to you what really happened. When I saw you there, it seemed like fate."

"Then I'm definitely not bringing you. I don't know how I'm going to explain this to Violet."

I was hoping Violet would bring a new guy to brunch, but no such luck. And for some reason, Grandma was intent on quizzing all the kids about their love life. Seems there weren't enough little kids in the family anymore and she was itching for some great-grandkids.

"Amanda, your mother told me you're seeing someone?" she asked.

I stuffed some ham in my mouth and nodded, hoping she'd move on to someone else.

"Is it serious?"

I shook my head no and she frowned, moving on to Violet.

Violet pouted. "Nope, no guys. Not since Pete."

"That's a shame. He seemed like a nice guy. So handsome, and— oh! He went on and on about my gravy."

Hey, I made the gravy, I thought.

Violet looked even more miserable and I wondered how long I could keep this a secret.

I skipped the Fourth of July barbecue with the family because I didn't want to bring Pete and I wasn't willing to miss the fireworks with him.

"You're going to have to tell your family sometime. I plan on sticking around," he said.

His words both thrilled and terrified me for a number of reasons. We kissed under the colorful show in the sky as I spun together visions of our future. I love Pete and I want to be with him forever. We spent a wonderful summer together and planned a vacation in the Caribbean together for October. Things were getting more and more serious.

We enjoyed a magnificent dinner right on the beach in Aruba on the last night of our trip. I was making mental notes for a new line of tropical tarts for the shop when Pete dropped to his knee and popped open a little, white box.

"Marry me, Amanda."

I didn't say yes. I couldn't. I just nodded and leapt into his arms. We kissed and celebrated until dawn.

"Guess this means I'm coming to Thanksgiving dinner with the Shepherds again."

Right. There was that little fly in the ointment to deal with.

I told my parents the big news, of course, and swore them to secrecy. Mom assured me everything would be okay, but I felt like a toad. Violet was going to hate me. She'd really been crazy about Pete. I knew how she felt. I'm crazy for him, too.

I made twice as many pies as usual and arrived at Grandma's door right before dinner with a major case of the butterflies. Pete squeezed my hand.

"It'll be fine. They loved me last year," he joked.

"They loved me, too. We're probably both going to get kicked out."

Grandpa Sam opened the door and squinted at Pete, but

apparently he didn't make the connection.

"We're just sitting down, kids. Grab a seat and give me those pies."

I unloaded the pies in the kitchen and took a deep breath before Pete and I walked out to the dining room. I heard a bunch of hellos, how are you doings, and who's your fellow? And then Violet's sudden intake of breath.

"Pete? You're dating Pete?" she asked.

There were a couple gasps around the table as memories caught up with the current situation.

Violet glared at me.

"Wasn't Pete your date last year, Violet?" Grandpa Sam asked, walking into the room eating a piece of pre-dinner pie.

"Yes."

"Oh," Grandpa said quietly.

Pete put his arm around me. "Actually, we're not just dating. We're engaged." I held out my hand and soon the room erupted in congratulations and hugs. But I saw Violet push back her chair and bolt from the room.

I figured she needed a moment to herself, so I sat down for dinner. Nothing tasted good. We've been friends since we were little, sharing many a sleepover. Our families even vacationed together a few times. We kind of lost touch as teenagers when we got busy with school, activities, and everything, but, still, it killed me to hurt her like this.

I served up dessert and went looking for Violet. She was in Grandma's guest room, looking through old photo albums. She looked up when I walked in and frowned.

"How long have you two been dating?"

I sat next to her on the bed. "Since Valentine's Day."

She did the math. "Not long after he broke up with me. I can't believe he dumped me for you." Her lip was wobbling.

There was a tap at the door and Pete was standing there.

Violet stiffened. "I do not want to see you. I should have known you were bad news. You broke up with me before Christmas and dumped her before prom. Wait, I thought you hated him for that," she said, looking at me.

"He explained a few things to me. He had a good reason for doing it."

Pete walked in. "I didn't have the money back in high school to take her. I always regretted losing her. When I saw her here at your party, it brought back a lot of memories. I didn't want to tell you the truth, that I was leaving you for your cousin, and I certainly I didn't want you to go out and buy me some fancy Christmas present. So, I broke up with you before the holiday. I'm sorry if the timing of it hurt you. I guess I'm not very good at the breakup thing."

"Which is why you better not do it again," Violet said. "Don't hurt my cousin. Be good to her." She pointed a threatening finger at him.

He put his arm around me and squeezed. "That's a promise I can make."

"We're okay?" I asked Violet.

She nodded. "Just don't make me a bridesmaid or anything."

"It's a deal. I have ghastly plans for the bridesmaid's dresses anyway."

Violet wasn't a bridesmaid in the wedding, as promised. I was thrilled to see her come to the ceremony with a good-looking date that couldn't keep his eyes off her. I made sure to toss the bouquet her way at the reception. She caught it and held it up victoriously. I gave her a thumbs-up and she crossed her fingers. The reception passed in a blur and the wedding of my dreams came to an end.

"So, does this make up for missing prom?" Pete teased, as we danced the last dance of the evening.

"I guess so." I laughed and kissed the boy who'd broken my heart so long ago.

THE END

WHAT BEGAN AS THE THANKSGIVING JINX
Now Feels A Lot Like Love!

Thanksgiving has always been more than a holiday in which to give thanks and consume lots of turkey. Thanksgiving, for me, was always a day of regret. Nothing good every happened to me on Thanksgiving. In fact, it became the day I most feared. It was that fear that drove me to become an agoraphobic—afraid to leave the house—and not wanting to be around anyone, including myself. It all started when I met Samuel.

My twin brother, Thomas, brought his coworker, Samuel, to Thanksgiving dinner. As soon as Samuel stepped in the door, I immediately noticed his gorgeous masculine stature. He was tall, about six feet-five, sun-kissed skin, with a lean muscular build. His eyes were light brown to match his light complexion. As we greeted one another, I noticed our handshake lasted longer than it should have. All during dinner, I felt him watching me. When I lifted my head from eating, and turned to look in his direction, he simply smiled at me—a warm radiant smile, which made my knees weak. A blush crept up my face.

After dinner and chatting, he left. I thought he would have asked for my number, but he didn't. Of course, knowing me, the chemistry I thought we had, could have been a figment of my imagination. I was never a size two; and consequently, men didn't really notice me.

A week after dinner, he called me. I didn't bother asking the stupid question, "How did you get my number?" because I knew my brother gave it to him. Our conversation was brief. There was no leisurely "get to know you" conversation. He called to make plans to see a movie, and at the end of our five-minute phone call, I had a date for dinner and a movie that weekend.

As we took our seats in the restaurant, he began the idle movie chit-chat, which always follows a movie date.

"So what did you think of the movie?"

"It was okay. The will to survive is something else. A little too stressful for me."

"Jamie, are you crazy. Duh, it's called human nature, animal instincts. The movie was great! Just okay? You must not have been watching the same movie or didn't understand it."

"It's just that I prefer dramas or comedies. I don't like horror, thrillers, sci-fi, or ultra violent movies."

I felt like I was defending myself, but I had already told him I didn't want to see the movie he picked out. But he didn't want to compromise, so we ended up watching it, anyway.

"Well, you'll just have to get over that, because those are all the categories I like. I don't plan on seeing any chick flicks."

I should have been incensed, but all I could hear was the hint of another date. I had never been on a second date before. I was the 'hit it and quit it' type. Since I never let anyone "hit it," they just left me alone. Guess I wasn't worth the effort.

He continued to talk, about the movie, politics, current events, his company, and his goals and future aspirations. He occupied most of the conversation. I nodded my head in agreement, and to indicate I was listening. It appeared that was all he required of the conversation. At the end of the night, he took me home. I thought that was the point where he would try to make his move sexually, but he didn't. He leaned over and gave me an ever so gentle kiss on the mouth. That was the end of our date, so I got out the car and went into my apartment.

Samuel and I dated for eight months, when he proposed during a romantic dinner (that I prepared) at his house. He walked across the table, pulled out a chair next to mine, reached for my hand, and held it gently.

"You know, I'm not getting any younger. You'd make a good wife for me. I think we are a good fit together. I make enough money that I could take care of you. And you know, of course, I love you. We should get married."

He opened a box and presented me with a gold ring with a three-quarter carat diamond.

He says he loves me, I thought. It definitely wasn't the most romantic proposal. He didn't even get down on one knee, but it was a proposal from a man whom I loved, who declared he loved me, and would take care of me. I accepted his proposal.

He wanted to get married on the one-year anniversary of the day we met. I worked frantically to plan a wedding in such a short amount of time. It helped that we were having a small ceremony with only about fifty people. I managed to pull it off; we were married on Thanksgiving. We had a lovely Thanksgiving themed ceremony with fall colors, and we served traditional Thanksgiving food.

After the ceremony and everyone was settled, I realized I had not eaten all day. Someone brought me a plate of food.

"You probably shouldn't eat, tonight. You wouldn't want to spill anything on that expensive gown, and look like a fool on your wedding day."

I looked into my new husband's eyes, and put my fork down. He had a point. Guess I wouldn't be eating until our honeymoon, I figured.

We were celebrating our first year of marriage at his parents' house, when my first stream of bad luck came. (At that moment I thought it was my first). I was sitting at the dinner table enjoying conversation with my in-laws when I felt a cramp. I figured it was the food, so I stopped eating. My mother in-law noticed the uncomfortable look on my face.

"Are you okay, darling?"

My husband heard his mother ask the question. He paused from his conversation with his father to turn and glance at me. He then turned back around and continued talking to his father.

"Uh, I don't know. I'm not feeling well at all." Another painful cramp came. "Maybe I could check your medicine cabinet and see if there is something I could take."

As I stood up, my mother-in- law gasped.

"Oh my God!"

There was blood in the seat and on my clothes. I had my first of several miscarriages.

Samuel prided himself on being able to have his wife stay at home. I didn't work. It was quite a boring life, as we had no kids to watch over. It didn't take that long to clean the house and cook dinner. To occupy my time, I took recreational classes like basket weaving, candle making, and jewelry making. I got really good at making jewelry and baskets. In fact, many of my friends would buy my jewelry and baskets. It was a nice side business, and it gave me something to do. It also gave me money that wasn't my husband's, and I enjoyed creating things with my own hands. My husband was not so happy with the idea.

"How could you insult me by selling jewelry to my friends? I have to work with some of these people. They will think we are broke and need the money. I told you those classes were stupid, and a waste of money. I let you take them when I shouldn't have. Didn't you even think what kind of message that would send?" He didn't give me time to respond. Instead he began yelling, "Of course not, you're too stupid and selfish! Don't sell to my friends, anymore."

He threw all of my jewelry on the floor and walked out of the room.

It had become tradition with us to spend Thanksgiving over his parents' house. I would always bring macaroni and cheese, string beans, and corn muffins. We had been married for ten years when one Thanksgiving, the tradition changed. He said his parents were going on vacation for Thanksgiving, and he wanted to use that opportunity to play catch up at the office. I tried not to feel hurt that he didn't want to spend the time with me during our anniversary. He said we could celebrate the upcoming weekend. My woman's intuition told me he was not going into the office. He was a hard worker, but not very dedicated. In the eleven years I had been with him, he went into the office on his day off a total of six times.

As he loved to say over the course of our relationship, he thought I was extremely stupid. However, I was smart enough to have noticed the telephone calls at late hours on the phone bill and the same number on his cell phone bill. I knew he was having an affair, but I kept telling myself it was just numbers, no real proof. That day, I decided I would get proof. I went on the Internet, typed in the mysterious phone number, and got a name and address. I got in my car and drove to that location. I pulled up to a small ranch house an hour outside of town. The lights were off, and it seemed no one was home. I decided to park a few houses up from her on the street and wait.

An hour later, my husband's car pulled up in front of the house. He parked the car, exited, and walked around to open the door for the woman. She was tall, medium build, with a dark complexion. He escorted her out of the car, closed the door behind her, and wrapped her in his arms for a searing, passionate kiss. He escorted her to the house. They both talked and laughed as they walked up the small incline to the front door. His jacket wrapped around her as if to protect her from the cold.

I don't know what angered or hurt me more: that he opened the car door for her, which he'd never done for me in eleven years—not even on our first date—that he gave her his jacket when she was cold, an act of kindness I was never afforded; that the simple kiss they shared held more passion than our whole marriage; or that he was giving to another woman all the things he never gave to me! I sat in the car, watched them go in the house together, and I cried.

That night when he came home, exhausted and satiated, I confronted him.

"Where were you?"

I sat up in bed with the lights on, watching him get undressed.

"I told you where I was. Are you deaf and stupid?"

"I saw you with her."

He paused from untying his tie. I thought he would deny the accusation, put the blame on me. Instead, he turned to look at me and replied, "I want a divorce. I thought you would make a good wife. I was wrong. I sold myself short. I don't love you, never have. You're stupid, fat, and unlovable, but you are a good cook."

The hurt I felt was indescribable. I ran from the bed to the bathroom and threw up. My life wasn't much, but he was all I had.

Somehow, throughout the course of our marriage, I became distant from my friends and family. He subtly, and not so subtly, took me away from them. Whenever I went to visit, he always had plans for us, or would make me feel guilty so I would have to cancel. As I hunched over the porcelain toilet, I could only think of the hurt and loneliness. I spent the rest of my ten-year anniversary crying in the downstairs bedroom, trying to figure out what a woman with basic education, no skills, and no money would do.

I moved in with my brother. I didn't want to go through the mental tug of war over money, alimony, ownership, and property with Samuel. In the end, we decided to sell all of the property and split the profits. I took one temp job after the next. I continued to make baskets and jewelry. I made more money doing that than I did temping. The Monday before Thanksgiving of the following year, my divorce was final.

My great grandfather bought land and built a cabin in the northern Georgia mountains. The family owned it and paid the taxes every year, but no one did anything with it. I asked to take over and move there, it met with no objection. I wanted to get away from everyone and everything. Thanksgiving was proving to be my Friday the 13th. I figured if I were alone when it came around, nothing bad would happen to me. I packed enough clothes, food, and jewelry and basket making supplies to last a month. I kept telling myself I was just going up there for Thanksgiving, but I had no intention of ever leaving.

When I got there, I cleaned the cabin, made one of the spare bedrooms an office, and the other one, a workroom for making my baskets and jewelry. I cooked, made beads and baskets, cleaned the master bedroom, and decorated it. After all was finished, I stretched across the bed, my head buried in the pillow, and cried. I cried for all that I had lost and all that I never had. I mourned for the loss of my children, miscarriages brought on by stress. I grieved for the wasted eleven years of my life married to a man who didn't love me.

I cried every night, and made jewelry and baskets everyday. I didn't have to worry about what people thought of me, if someone would criticize me, or anything happening to me because it was just me. When it came time to leave, I couldn't. I was supposed to only stay up there for a week—two at the most. I opened the door to leave and froze.

The "real world" didn't seem as enticing as it once did. In my youth, all I wanted was a chance to grow up and live in the real world. Standing in the doorway, I craved that innocence, before experience, life, and marriage, broke my spirit. I thought about all the things that could happen once I left, and the chances of running into Samuel, or his new lover, having to keep jumping from one temp job to the next, or finding another man like Samuel. In the real world, I was a divorcee, lonely, and had nothing. I closed the door on the real world, and retreated to my sanctuary.

I managed to find a way to make a living and eat, without leaving the cabin. Before I left, my brother had created a website for me, displaying my jewelry and baskets. That is how most of my orders came in. Living in a small town and classifying myself as a small business, I was able to get postal pickup at my door. The grocery store had a boy that delivered. My brother bought the rest of my things to the cabin. My family would come to visit. I could see how they wanted to get me to leave, but there was nothing they could say to make me change my mind.

About two months into my solitude, I was on the computer checking my orders and doing inventory when I got a very peculiar instant message.

It was addressed to "Hello Beautiful Smile."

I didn't have a personals ad up, and I didn't know who the person was. The IM screen said it was from H. Baxter.

Hello there. Do I know you?

It's not like I was busy, I was curious who H. Baxter was.

No. I'm in the small business group. I saw your profile.

I was in an online community for small business owners. I was pretty active in the group, always asking questions, posting my comments, and networking. I figured he had checked my profile. I posted a face shot with me wearing several pieces I had made. My thinking was it was a good picture to advertise my business as well as say who I was. I was guilty of doing the same thing. Whenever someone responded to a post, I would click on their profile to see what their small business was, and what they looked like.

Thanks for the compliment.

No problem, r u single?

I couldn't believe a strange man . . . well I hoped it was a man, was trying to virtually pick me up. I went to close out of my instant messenger, but then I figured it's not real, it's virtual, what would a little chat hurt.

Newly single and you?

Single, so what idiot messed up and let you go?

I tapped my fingers on the keyboard, having pondered that same question, since Samuel declared he wanted a divorce. The difference between his question and mine, I always pondered what I did wrong. I didn't want to answer, still feeling the hurt from Samuel's betrayal. I looked at my screen for stretched moments of time, thinking. My new buddy thought I had left.

You still there?

111

I typed a quick response to let him know I was. I exhaled, thinking of the animosity of the chat world, and answered him honestly.

My ex-husband left me for another woman. He was the first man to genuinely show interest in me. You saw my picture I'm no size two.

He interrupted me. Yeah, I saw your picture . . . You're gorgeous!

And there it was, at thirty-three, my first compliment on my appearance. I blushed from the bottom of my feet to the top of my head. Insults I knew how to take, compliments were foreign territory to me. I decided to quickly acknowledge him and continue with my story.

Uh thanks, but not everyone feels that way.

Another interruption, including you?

That was the million-dollar question. How did I feel about myself? I knew I had not been happy with the reflection in the mirror since I could remember. I would shrug it off, and I decided it I kept lying to myself saying I was beautiful, one day I might believe the lie. It never happened.

I don't know. Maybe I do. Who knows?

I avoided conversations about me like the black plague. It was my least favorite subject.

Well, I know. You're beautiful. You need to see yourself like I do. Sorry to cut you off, please finish your story about your stupid ex-husband.

The kindest words ever spoken to me came from a stranger over the Internet. I continued my story of meeting, marrying, and subsequently, divorcing Samuel. This led to him describing his last relationship. Apparently, we had more in common than a desire to create a small business—we had both been cheated on. I was left by my husband for another woman, and he was left by his fiancé for her first love, for whom she married two months after their breakup. We moved on to more casual topics of current events, favorite movies, political standing, and religious affiliation. He was Catholic; I was Episcopalian. When I started yawning profusely, I looked at the clock on the computer, and realized it was past two in the morning. My eyes couldn't stay open, so I ended our four-hour conversation, and we said our good nights.

Oh, by the way, my name is Henry.

My name is Jamie. Good night, Henry.

Good night, beautiful.

I went to bed with thoughts of Henry and our conversations. As I drifted off to sleep, I tried to conjure Henry's image in my head. I couldn't because I didn't know what he looked like. It was something I planned to correct during our next chat session. That night, I fell asleep with a smile on my face.

I woke up the next morning with thoughts of Henry on my mind, our conversation, the way he made me feel. I wanted to rush to the computer to see if he was online. Realizing I was turning a bit obsessive, I decided instead to shower and fill a few orders. The day went by very slowly. I'm certain if my computer was in the same room as my supply/work room, I would have given up all pretenses and stared at the computer until Henry logged on.

Nighttime came, and I logged onto my e-mail and my instant messenger. I sat at the computer and checked e-mails, sent confirmations, and participated in online group discussions for hours—no Henry. When midnight arrived, I decided to log off and go lie in bed, and watch TV. As I clicked the button that would take me to the sign-on screen, a message appeared.

Hello, Beautiful. Glad to see you're still up.

I let out a deep sigh, I didn't' realize I was holding my breath until his instant message appeared. Henry and I chatted for hours— that night and every night—for the following three weeks. Our first separation in chatting came when he had to go to the Reserves one weekend.

The night before he left to go to the Reserves, we talked about setting up websites and minor issues he was having in setting up his business. Since I was home all day, I had plenty of time to read and learn many of the ins and outs.

Brains and beauty; what a killer package. You really are special.

He always seemed to make me blush. As usual, I didn't know how to respond so I ignored the comment and continued answering his website question.

Anyway if you type in the—

He interrupted my explanation.

Why do you do that?

Perplexed, I answered, Do what?

Brush me off or change the subject every time I give you a compliment?

Oh, I didn't realize I was doing it. I'm just not used to them, I guess. Samuel never gave them to me. Whereas I know my parents love me and took care of me, they weren't big on compliments or positive reinforcement.

There was a long pause. I thought my confession turned him off. Men liked confident females. I had definitely grown to the love myself more, but I had a long way to go to become a confident female.

Sorry, all of that happened, but I am not Samuel and I'm not your parents. You need to start getting used to compliments, because I plan on giving them to you every chance I get. I have to go need a good night sleep for Reserves, tomorrow. Good night, beautiful.

That weekend, I managed to get a lot of work done and catch up on my sleep. The weekend felt long and lonely. I was missing my nightly chats with Henry. Monday slowly crept in. As was my morning ritual, I woke up and checked my e-mail and orders. An e-mail from H. Baxter grabbed my attention. I noticed it had an attachment. I opened the e-mail.

Toni Braxton had seven days, but for me it's just been two.

It doesn't change the fact that baby, I miss you.

Stay beautiful. Talk to you, tonight

Henry

Reading his poem, referencing the songstress Toni Braxton, I was smiled from ear to ear. I clicked on the attachment, and saw the face of an angel. Henry sent me his picture. He fit his description, perfectly. He did not lie about any detail. Henry was the most attractive man I had seen, because I had gotten to know who he was on the inside.

Like clockwork, Henry logged in at 11:23 p.m. He worked evening shifts at the plant, spent his days taking classes, and spent his nights chatting with me. I don't know where he found the time to sleep. We were having our normal idle chit-chat when, in one simple line, he changed the boundaries of our relationship.

Can I call you?

I quickly gave him my number. He indicated he would call me in five minutes. I ran around the cabin like a chicken with my head cut off. I brushed my teeth, straightened my clothes, and fixed a glass of water. I was acting as if any moment he would appear at the door, instead of receiving a simple phone call.

As promised, he called me in exactly five minutes. When I answered the phone I was winded, but I tried to sound sexy. My resulting phone greeting was that of an asthmatic. The deep baritone timbre of his voice as he responded, "Hello sexy," sent chills up my spine. He told me how good it was to finally talk to me after so much chatting. He said I sounded better than he ever could have imagined. We both enjoyed moving our Internet affair to the phone. It made it more real. When I began chatting with Henry, I did so because it wasn't real to me. After getting to know him, all I wanted was for it to be real.

Henry and I talked every night for several months. We often spoke of what we would do once we met each other. Some nights, that innocent topic would turn into phone sex. I would glide my hands across my body as I listened to him describe what he would do to me. I would close my eyes as envision us being together, riding the waves of passion—arriving on the shores of ecstasy in heated bliss. As we arrived to that heated bliss in my mind, so would I arrive in my bed on the phone with Henry.

114

I was almost ashamed to admit that the best relationship in my life was with a man I had never met. His busy schedule kept him in California, and my fear kept me in my North Georgia cabin.

"So what are you doing this Labor Day weekend?"

Although Henry knew about my agoraphobia, he asked me the same question every holiday since we started chatting just before Martin Luther King Day. My answer was always, "Nothing, catching up on orders and making jewelry." I was tired of giving the same answer. I was tired of the self-loathing and fear. That time, my answer was different.

"I think I am going to surprise my brother and his wife. Maybe convince them to have a Labor Day barbeque in my honor."

"I'm so proud of you. Brains, beauty, and bravery."

"Don't forget butt. I have brains, beauty, bravery, and a nice butt."

From the throaty grunt he gave in response to my comment, I knew he was visualizing my nice butt. Feeling the conversation was on the verge of turning erotic, I quickly interrupted his thoughts.

"Sorry, you won't be here to greet me when I open the door."

"Me too, baby. You just keep opening that door and stepping into the world. One day, I'll be on the other side, ready to hold you in my arms and show you how much I love you. And Jamie, I do love you."

I don't know how it happened, but in the middle of everything, I fell in love.

"I love you too, Henry."

Labor Day weekend arrived. I packed a small carry-on luggage, collected my keys that I hadn't used in almost a year, and opened my front door. I expected to feel fear or reluctance, but I didn't. I stepped outside and inhaled the scent of freedom—freedom from fear and loneliness. When I exhaled, I released my doubts and insecurities. I walked to the car feeling better than I had in years. I knew I owed my new outlook to Henry. Hearing him constantly tell me I was smart and beautiful, among many other things, I began to believe it and tell myself the exact same things.

My brother was shocked and ecstatic to see me. He hugged me so tight, I felt I would pass out. I had to tell him I couldn't breathe so he would release me.

The family did decide to have a barbeque in my honor. I was sent to the store to purchase a few items they had forgotten. As I glided down the sauce aisle looking for ketchup, I saw Samuel with a woman (not the one I had caught him with on Thanksgiving) perusing meat selections. He noticed me and whispered something to his female companion. She moved the cart further down the meat aisle, out of sight, and he approached me.

"Well, I see the hermit has come out of hiding."

I simply stared at him, feeling it best not to feed into his taunts and cause a scene. Of course, since Samuel's idea of conversation was someone listening to him talk, I didn't have to wait long for him to continue.

"Did you go into hiding because of me or because you couldn't find a job? I mean with no one to support you, no brains, and no skills what else could you do?"

He was baiting me, and I knew it.

"Actually, I wasn't in hiding at all. Hiding implies no one knew where I was, and that I didn't want to be found."

He interrupted me.

"Yes, I know what hiding means. . . ."

"I'm still talking. Try shutting up and listening."

He was taken aback by my aggressiveness. I assumed he was shocked silent, because he didn't say anything else.

"As I was saying . . . I wasn't in hiding. And, no I don't have a job." He didn't interrupt, but I saw his self-satisfied smirk. I didn't pay him any attention and continued my story.

"I have my own business, and it makes a pretty nice income."

I tapped my fingers on my chin and looked up as if in deep thought. "In fact, I make more than you ever brought home. I make my own hours. I do what I love, so it's not a job. So how is your job going?"

I already knew he had been laid off as a result of company downsizing. Judging by the evil look he gave me, he knew I knew.

"My wife and I are doing fine."

I recognized the purpose of that statement was to make me jealous. Instead, I felt sorry for his wife. I nodded my head, and with a genuine smile, bade him good-bye.

"I'm glad to hear that Samuel. Treat her well, Sammy. Best of luck to the both of you."

I continued my journey down the aisle, signifying our conversation was over.

It was in that moment I realized he no longer had any power over me. I decided to move back to Atlanta. I wanted to be gone by Thanksgiving, so I could spend it with my family. I found an apartment in the city, and decided to use the cabin to store all my supplies and back orders. My last day in the cabin was the night before Thanksgiving. I decided to leave early Thanksgiving morning to avoid traffic. I talked to Henry on my last night, and gave him all of my new contact information.

As planned, I woke up early that morning, and got the last remnants of my personal belongings. I turned to take one last look at my former sanctuary, and opened the door to leave. Henry was standing on the steps holding a bouquet of three-dozen red roses. The man of my dreams was on my doorsteps. I dropped my things, and ran into his arms. Thankfully, he had the foresight to lay the roses on the stoop, so I would not crush them and get poked with the thorns. I was swallowed in the strength of his embrace. I cried in his arms, happy that this day had finally arrived. I felt drops of dampness on my forehead as we were both swept away in the emotion of the moment.

Henry followed me to Atlanta. The next day, we had Thanksgiving dinner at my brother's house. Henry and I spent every Thanksgiving after that together as husband and wife, and later on as Mom and Dad to our twin daughters.

Somewhere between starting my family and recreating my Thanksgiving, I learned its true meaning. Thanksgiving was about being thankful for family, love, experiences, and healthy relationships—with myself and other people.

THE END

www.ingramcontent.com/pod-product-compliance
Lightning Source LLC
Chambersburg PA
CBHW071402170626
46811CB00003B/1235